"It's your ba[...] say in how he or she is raised."

Harvey scrubbed a hand down his face. "So you're keeping it?"

The thought of not seeing this pregnancy through hadn't even crossed her mind. From the moment she'd read the results of that first pregnancy test— and the five after—she'd known her decision. There wasn't anything more important to Drennan. She would sleep with a hundred strangers in bars to make it happen. A surge of defensiveness arced through her. "Yes."

"All right. I'll help. Clothes, college, braces, even your doctor appointments, I'll support him or her. If you want me to pay child support and have a lawyer draft up an agreement, I'll sign it, but I'm not interested in being a father. Understand? I don't want custody, and I don't want to be involved." Harvey stepped into her, close enough to touch, and lowered his voice. "When it comes to raising this baby, you're on your own."

A DROWNING
IN EMERALD POOL

NICHOLE SEVERN

Harlequin

INTRIGUE

MIX
Paper | Supporting responsible forestry
FSC® C021394

To the readers who love grumpy heroes.

This one's for you.

ISBN-13: 978-1-335-69062-3

A Drowning in Emerald Pool

Copyright © 2026 by Natascha Jaffa

Harlequin Enterprises ULC
22 Adelaide St. West, 41st Floor
Toronto, Ontario M5H 4E3, Canada
www.Harlequin.com

HarperCollins Publishers
Macken House, 39/40 Mayor Street Upper,
Dublin 1, D01 C9W8, Ireland
www.HarperCollins.com

Printed in Lithuania

Nichole Severn writes explosive romantic suspense with strong heroines, heroes who dare challenge them and a hell of a lot of guns. She resides with her very supportive and patient husband, as well as her demon spawn, in Utah. When she's not writing, she's constantly injuring herself running, rock climbing, practicing yoga and snowboarding. She loves hearing from readers through her website, www.nicholesevern.com, and on Facebook at nicholesevern.

Books by Nichole Severn

Harlequin Intrigue

Red Rock Murders

Manhunt in the Narrows
Disappearance at Angel's Landing
Murder at Lava Point
A Drowning in Emerald Pool

New Mexico Guard Dogs

K-9 Security
K-9 Detection
K-9 Shield
K-9 Guardians
K-9 Confidential
K-9 Justice

Defenders of Battle Mountain

Grave Danger
Dead Giveaway
Dead on Arrival
Presumed Dead
Over Her Dead Body
Dead Again

Visit the Author Profile page at Harlequin.com.

CAST OF CHARACTERS

Harvey Knight—This national park ranger is ready to arrest a hiker swimming in one of Zion's most protected natural pools, only to discover the body of a drowning victim instead. His military service has prepared him for every scenario—except the responding assistant medical examiner claiming she's pregnant with his baby.

Drennan Hawes—Her former life as a trauma emergency room physician blew up in her face. No one in the ME's office knows how much of a failure she's become, and she wants to keep it that way. Until one night with a stranger results in a surprise pregnancy that has her craving the family she's always wanted. But convincing the father of her baby to want the same future is proving more difficult than solving the homicide investigation keeping them together.

Ellender Garza—She's hiding a secret the killer can't afford to have exposed...

Zion National Park—Two hundred and thirty-two square miles of trails, red rock and danger waiting to happen.

Chapter One

Two pink lines.

Over ten days late.

Assistant medical examiner Drennan Hawes stared at the stick until those lines blurred into one. If she stared long enough, maybe she could convince herself it wasn't true. She wasn't pregnant. But then another round of nausea forced her to her knees, and she lost everything she'd eaten at breakfast.

Okay. She was pregnant.

Oh, hell. What was she going to tell her mother? Drennan pressed a hand to her forehead as she flushed the toilet and pressed her back against the wall. She could already hear the criticism clawing its way into her brain. All that education and she'd gone and gotten knocked up like an impulsive teenager.

She should've stayed in Ohio like her mother had wanted. None of this would've happened if she'd just listened for once. It didn't matter that taking this job with the medical examiner's office in Hurricane, Utah, had been the escape she'd needed or that staying in the same place that'd broken her over and over would've eventually turned her into a bitter, toxic thing like her mother. Athena Hawes knew best.

A sick sensation that had nothing to do with morning sickness flooded through her. Her skin turned clammy.

Worse. What would she tell the father? *How* would she tell him? They'd parted that night without exchanging names or contact information. For all she knew, he'd only been passing through, visiting the park on a weekend with friends. Though she guessed being in that bar could've made him a local. It certainly had been off the beaten path and not as popular as some of the other bars in town. Blood drained from her face and neck until it felt like it was pooling in her feet. She couldn't move, couldn't think. Their one night together wasn't supposed to be anything more than a bit of selfish fun. Now they were having a baby? After years of following the plan that'd been strategically put in place for her since kindergarten, she'd buckled under the endless pressure to succeed, achieve, do more. She'd quit her job at the hospital, stopped answering her friends' calls and messages and quietly disappeared from the life she'd spent decades building for herself.

A mental breakdown, her therapist had said. Utterly disappointing, her mother had said. Couldn't even stand to look at her. What good was a trauma physician who couldn't keep her patients alive?

And Drennan had realized it then. That no amount of overachieving or money would earn her mother's love. That possibility had died a long time ago. All she could do was run. Escape. Her search for a new job—a new life—had come in the form of an assistant medical examiner position in the middle of nowhere Utah. A job where she couldn't call the wrong shots, her patients were already dead and no one knew the dumpster fire that her life had become. Her mom's angry voicemails and demands laced with cutting threats had dwindled in the four months since she'd bought out her apartment lease, packed up her car with everything she owned apart from furniture and headed straight toward the sunset. But not entirely.

It'd been one of those voicemails—it'd taken weeks of practice to silence her mother's calls—that had driven her to the hole-in-the-wall bar in Springdale, the tiny tourist town right outside Zion National Park. That night with a handsome stranger who couldn't seem to take his eyes off her had helped in forgetting what a screwup she'd become. For once, she'd chosen herself rather than some out of reach level of approval.

Drennan's hand shook as she checked the test for the two hundredth time. She tapped her head back against the wall. "And here is your reward."

She was going to have a baby.

Her phone rang from the nightstand in her bedroom, and Drennan forced herself to her feet. Acid coated the inside of her mouth, but whoever was calling wouldn't notice, and she rounded into her small bedroom. She'd done a lot of work in making it feel homey without being able to paint. Lots of hanging green plants, dark bedding and macramé accents. She'd set up a reading chair where she spent most nights trying not to doom scroll, but being on call 24-7 kept her tied to her phone more than she wanted. Still, it was worth it, the peace she'd found here surrounded by red rock, rolling desertscapes and mountains that seemed to pierce the sky. The opposite of Ohio in every way. Drennan slid her thumb across the screen as the office's phone number scrolled. "Dr. Hawes."

"We've got a body." Iain Yarrow didn't bother with pleasantries. In fact, she was pretty sure the older medical examiner who'd hired her had a phobia of small talk, but it was one of the reasons she loved working for him.

Straight to the point, direct without any manipulation or lies and always calm. Another opposite of Ohio. "National park rangers called it in about five minutes ago. A drowning from what they can tell."

There went her plan to cry over her stupidity in forgetting to stay on top of her birth control with all the changes she'd undergone in the past few months. She checked her smartwatch, one of those new ones she decided to splurge on with her massive severance from the hospital. Only to realize she probably should've saved that money. Because now she'd need to buy supplies—for a baby. A crib, for one thing.

Drennan scanned her bedroom. The one-bedroom apartment wasn't big enough. Where was she supposed to put it? No. She couldn't think about that right now. She had a job she very much wanted to keep. "Okay. I can be at the office in about ten minutes."

Though she couldn't really call the basement of Metland Mortuary an office. Desert far outweighed population in Southern Utah. With a hundred different small pockets of people peppered throughout the lower half of the state, there was no real need for each town to have its own medical examiner or coroner, an oversize hospital complete with a morgue or an entire building dedicated to the medical examiner's office. Their office in Hurricane—pronounced Hur-i-can, as she'd learned the hard way—served their local population, the tourist town of Springdale and Zion National Park with just one medical examiner and now an assistant. She and Dr. Yarrow were the only staff, acting as rulers of their too-small kingdom covering an exam room lined with cabinets, a single stainless steel exam table and a wall of narrow, horizontal refrigerators to house their patients. The funeral home director also had access considering it was his building, much to the detriment of Drennan being able to do her job in a timely manner most of the time.

"You won't be assisting me this time." Static or movement—she couldn't tell—filtered through Dr. Yarrow's end of the line. "I'm in the middle of a priority autopsy. I need you at the scene to take custody of the remains."

The scene? Nerves and another dose of nausea shot through her. "I've never visited a scene."

"There's not much to it. Mostly preliminary stuff." The medical examiner's voice echoed through the line. She could clearly picture him standing over their exam table with his tape recorder—old-school and inefficient—picking up every word of their current conversation. "Photograph the body and the surrounding scene, make sure no one has moved or touched anything, get information from whoever found the body and load it up to bring it back to the office. Ask the rangers on the scene for help."

Sounded easy enough, but Drennan's nerves wouldn't settle. Despite the months since becoming a Utahn, she had yet to set foot inside Zion National Park. There just hadn't been an opportunity. From the photos that'd come up on her search for a new life, the park was nothing short of heaven, with a river cutting straight through, mile-high red rock views and winding scenic drives through acres of wilderness. She'd always planned to visit. Guess today was as good a time as any. "All right. I'll call you if there are any issues."

Grabbing her gear at the door, Drennan jogged down the stairs from her second-story apartment and collapsed behind the wheel of her SUV. She hit the park's toll entrance within thirty minutes after switching her SUV for the ME van, lining up behind a rush of visitor vehicles, and her stomach flipped. "You cannot throw up in the car."

She wasn't sure if she was talking to herself or the tiny bundle of cells dividing in her uterus at an alarming rate.

The promise of fall nipped at her exposed skin as she hit the window power button and showed her credentials to the ranger behind the dark booth glass. "I'm responding to a call one of your rangers made to the ME's office."

The ranger directed her to park at the visitor's center, board the shuttle and make her way to the Grotto, the trailhead that would take her to the Emerald Pools trail where the body had been discovered. Hikers, families and selfie-obsessed visitors geared with backpacks, hats and sunscreen bumped and tossed her in the herd as they departed the shuttle. It took a few breaths of exhaust-tainted air for her to get her bearings. The Grotto acted as a nerve center for hikers to access several trails from one location, with Emerald Pools located across the asphalted one-lane road and over a man-made slat bridge. Impossibly tall trees added a bit of shade and brought her temperature down a couple degrees, but it wouldn't last long with the sun angling into the vast canyon that made up the park. It seemed she couldn't stop sweating as her body adjusted to the rush of pregnancy hormones, and she was little more than eight weeks along from her calculations. Things were about to get so much worse.

The trail entrance had been roped off. Clearly the rangers had enough sense to limit access to the scene where the body had been discovered. Another flash of her ME credentials got her through the barrier, and she started up the winding—sometimes too narrow—switchbacks leading to the lower, mid and upper pools, gear in hand. Her breath sawed in and out of her chest, her heart rate too high. Damn, she felt as though she'd run a marathon. Part of that was the pregnancy—yay for unending, bone-grinding exhaustion—and the other part was the altitude. Her body wasn't used to thriving on less oxygen yet.

After what felt like more than an hour—honestly, how much farther did she have to climb?—Drennan reached the lower pool. Well, more of a dying stream. Beautiful, as expected, with moss-lined water cutting across the rocks before diving over the ledge into the green pool below. Evidence of a rockslide broke up the smooth lines of natural architecture, but she couldn't linger to study why. The middle pool, located farther up the trail, was much deeper, though smaller and less impressive than she'd expected. Dead branches and mud caked the edges draining down the mountain.

It was the upper pool, which required every ounce of energy and some ankle-rolling, winding maneuvers to reach, that took her breath away. A sheer cliff protected the sprawling emerald-color water in layers of jagged red rock, black stains and a flowing waterfall that sprayed against her face with every gust of wind. Drennan stood stunned at the beauty, forgetting entirely why she'd had to haul herself up this mountain in the first place.

"I take it you're here for the body." The deep, very male voice resonated through her a split second before familiar glacial-blue eyes registered. Instant recognition flared across the ranger's bearded, handsome face as she turned to face him. His entire body stiffened as though he expected a fight. "You."

Drennan took in his uniform, complete with the National Park Ranger badge sewed across his broad chest—none of which he'd been wearing the night they'd met eight weeks ago—and her throat went dry. He was exactly as she'd remembered. Towering, muscular but honed in a lethal way rather than bulky with guarded dark eyes. Her nerves got the best of her this time. "I'm pregnant."

Chapter Two

He couldn't have heard her right.

National Park Ranger Harvey Knight forced himself a step back as though he could rewind time. He'd spent his morning pulling a body from the upper pool, but those two little words threatened to unleash a mountain of emotion he'd locked away for good reason. None of this made sense. What was she even doing here? Uneven ground around the natural pond caught at the edge of his heel, throwing off his balance. But it was his head he couldn't get straight. "I'm sorry. What are you even doing here? How did you get through the rangers at the trail entrance?"

Distinct lines deepened between perfectly shaped brows that matched the dark blond of her hair. Hell, she was just as beautiful as he remembered, with those wide green eyes framed by the darkest lashes he'd ever seen. Even dressed in a plain sweatshirt and jeans with tennis shoes she somehow wiped his memory of any other woman he'd been with. He could still feel the press of her mouth against his from that night two months ago, remember what it felt like to have her in his hands. The sounds she'd made beneath his sheets as they worked to forget reality. For one night, he'd been able to ignore the rage that'd driven him to that bar in the first place. Because of her. They'd parted without so much as exchanging first names, and Harvey had resigned himself to never feeling that kind of intensity with another human being again. There hadn't been use for words, empty promises or plans. That night had simply become two people who'd found each other in a moment of need. A once in a lifetime encounter he hadn't been able to stop thinking about since he'd walked her to her car and watched her drive away.

She grabbed for the lanyard around her neck, showcasing a washed-out photo of herself, though he couldn't focus enough to catch any of the information stamped into the reflective surface. "I got a call about a body. I'm here from the medical examiner's office."

"*You're* the medical examiner." His shock put a disbelieving twist on his tone he hadn't meant to sound as offensive as it did. Damn it. He had to get ahold of himself, but, if he was being honest, this woman was the last person he expected to show up at this scene.

"Assistant medical examiner." A hardness that didn't belong overtook her expression as she transferred a duffel bag—presumably full of gear—from one hand to the other. At nearly a whole head shorter than his six-three, she leveled him with a look that could strip paint. "Drennan Hawes. Did you hear what I said a minute ago?"

I'm pregnant. The news rushed back and nearly plowed him over. Gravity intensified until he was sure he'd become nothing more than a pile of blood and tissue if it went on long enough. Scraping a hand down his face, Harvey swiped at the thin layer of water coming off the falls to his left. "How?"

"What?" She cut that brilliant gaze matching the color of the pool to him.

"How are you pregnant?" This wasn't happening.

They'd had the discussion beforehand. They both tested clean during their last physicals and took precautions. He hadn't gone to that bar with the intention of sharing his bed that night, but he wasn't reckless, either. They'd been careful. "You told me you were on birth control."

Drennan—her name was Drennan, because of course everything he'd learned about her fit just as perfectly—lowered her voice, as though suddenly aware they weren't the only officials on a death scene. "I was. I *am*."

"Knight, we've got to get a move on." The head ranger of law enforcement division, a man who resembled a WWE wrestler more than an outdoorsman, wound one finger in a circle to hurry him up. Ranger Murray Simpson wasn't big on patience.

"This isn't the time." Slipping his hand between her rib cage and elbow, he gripped her arm, dragging her away from prying ears. And, damn it all to hell, that was a mistake. Hints of her perfume—the same scent that'd clung to his pillows and sheets in the days after their encounter—caught at the back of his throat. It'd faded after a while, but his body had somehow become accustomed to the light citrus scent. He hadn't been able to sleep for weeks, going as far as to try to hunt down that particular perfume just so he could get some damn sleep. Only now he realized it was all her. Natural and unobtainable. "I have a body on one of our most popular trails, and the superintendent is breathing down our necks to get Emerald Pools reopened as soon as possible. We'll talk about this later."

He added the much-needed distance between them, careful not to throw off her balance as he released his hold, and headed for the small grouping of rangers hovering over the body he'd found face down in the pond a little more than two hours ago.

"Are you the ranger who called it in?" Drennan's voice cut through the buzz of panic, more distant than a moment ago, as she raced to catch up to him.

He'd offended her. Hell. His fantasies of coming into contact with her again had gone out the window the second she'd opened her mouth. Harvey slowed his escape but fought the urge to take her gear to ease her effort. Pregnant. Son of a bitch. He didn't know how to act around a pregnant woman. He'd been an only child of miserable parents and practically raised himself. No cousins or nieces or nephews to help with. Kids, having a family, a wife, had never been in the stars after the way he'd witnessed his mother take insult after insult. Not to mention the bruises that'd followed. His path had led him straight into the military. As far from home as possible. "Guess neither of us were interested in exchanging names. Harvey Knight."

Harvey shut down the urge to extend his hand. Considering how they'd spent their first meeting, they were well past formal introductions. "I found the body a little after seven this morning on my patrol route. The park is open 24-7, so it's hard to tell how long she's been up here. My guess is between sunset last night and early this morning. The last shuttle coming down from Temple of Sinawava heads back to the visitor's center at 7:15 p.m. Most hikers make sure they're back at the trailhead before then."

He pulled to a stop outside the duo of rangers guarding and studying the remains as if they knew a damn thing about what to do. They parted at his approach, revealing the woman he'd pulled from the pool. Positioned on her back, the drowning victim stared back with nothing but emptiness in her expression. "She was face down when I found her. Fully clothed and geared up."

Drennan—he wanted to roll her name over in his mind

a thousand times—dropped her gear then crouched beside it. Pulling what looked like a dark blue windbreaker from inside, she threaded her legs into a full-length bodysuit. Bright yellow letters announced her as a representative of the ME's office as she zipped up the front of the bodysuit and snapped into a pair of latex gloves. Next came a camera she wound around her neck with a thick strap meant to handle a good amount of weight. She snapped an initial photo of the body then checked the viewfinder. "How deep is the water?"

A gust of wind whipped another layer of water at their small grouping and splattered it across the face of their victim.

"A few feet at its deepest." Harvey set his hands on his hips, not really sure where to go from here. The law enforcement rangers retained jurisdiction in cases like this, but Simpson had wanted him here to answer questions for the medical examiner. "We warn hikers not to go in because of the algae and moss that can make the rocks under the surface unstable, but sometimes they're more interested in getting the perfect selfie than paying attention to their safety."

A never-ending endeavor to keep people alive from their own ignorance.

If their victim had slipped, her phone or camera could be lost to the pool. It'd take time the superintendent wasn't really willing to give them to fish it out. The victim's skin had taken on a waxy pallor, pale and smooth, with some bloating compromising her once thin features. No bruises as far as he could tell, but Harvey knew better than most that some people were capable of violence that couldn't be seen to the human eye. He didn't even know what he was doing here. He was a regular trail ranger who worked his shifts five days a week and went home, and right now, this body was keeping him from doing just that. He was just the unlucky bastard who'd found the poor woman.

"Who all has touched the body?" Drennan shifted to a new angle and took another photo of the remains, once again checking the viewfinder as though she didn't trust herself with the results. Then again, what did he really know about her other than a single night of sex and a claim she was carrying his baby?

The muscles in his jaw ached under the pressure of his back teeth. She seemed to go out of her way not to look at him, to treat him like any other ranger, keeping her tone neutral and distant. She obviously wasn't happy with the way their conversation had gone, but what had she expected him to say at hearing the news they were having a kid? Harvey dug his fingertips into his sides as that familiar anger tried to bust through his control. "Nobody. Just me."

"How did you pull her from the water? Where did you touch her?" Toeing the thin line between the end of her tennis shoes and the victim's body, Drennan shoved her hands into the victim's jacket, coming up empty, then moved on to the next pocket.

"By her jacket." As much as he hated the third degree, she was doing her job. He had to remember that. "I wasn't really keen on touching her anywhere else."

Pulling the woman's backpack free of both arms, the assistant medical examiner who'd barged into his life not once but twice in the past two months handed off the bag to him. "Let's see if we can find an ID. My office can take care of next of kin notifications if you need."

"I'll take care of it." Harvey didn't know Ranger Simpson well, but from what he'd heard, the man took every case of his personally. It wasn't any surprise he'd volunteered to make the call. Simpson searched every section of the bag, setting out a water bottle, a handful of snacks and sunscreen. "No ID or phone. It's possible they're at the bottom of the pool."

"In most cases of drowning I've come across, we can get an ID from dental or DNA. Fingerprints will take a couple days of dehydrating the skin on her fingers, but I'll keep in touch with any updates our office has for you. I'll need help getting her to my van at the visitor's center." Letting her camera drop to her stomach by the strap around her neck, Drennan shoved herself to a standing position, then tipped to one side. Her hand shot out, meeting nothing but air.

Harvey rushed forward before she hit the ground. He caught her around the middle as both other rangers moved in for support. All too aware of how perfectly she fit against him. "Are you okay?"

"Fine. Thanks." Her exhale tickled along his jaw and reinvigorated his senses with that hint of perfume. Righting herself, Drennan shook her head. "Guess I'm just not used to the elevation out here yet."

She pulled a folded black bag from her duffel bag of tricks. Throwing out one end, she laid it parallel to the body, zipper side up. "I have what I need from the remains for now. I'll get her back to Hurricane to assist Dr. Yarrow with the autopsy in the next couple of days and send any findings to your law enforcement division."

"Don't you need to clear that with her family first?" A restlessness flooded through him at the idea of her walking out of here after without another word. Some small part of him wasn't willing to leave them in this distant, emotionless, professional emptiness they'd found. Though Harvey knew that was exactly what he should do.

"Not when a death is considered suspicious. You see this thin layer of foam around the victim's mouth?" Drennan crouched beside the body, pointing to a collection of froth he'd assumed had come from buildup at the waterfall's base. "It's called hemorrhagic edema fluid. Mucus in the body mixes with the water in her lungs. She was alive when she went into that water. Considering the lack of blunt force trauma to her head, the depth of the water and the weight of her pack, she should've been able to stand on her own two feet to get out. But these bruises on the back of her neck?" She shifted the victim's hair out of the way, displaying a clear outline of a handprint spanning the waxy skin. "They tell me she was murdered."

Chapter Three

She couldn't stop her hands from shaking.

Drennan slammed the door to the van closed, sealing the young woman from the emerald pool inside. It'd taken all four of them to get her remains down the trail and a whole lot of maneuvering on the narrower edges of the switchbacks, but they'd done it in less than an hour. She'd had to record the temperature of the water the victim had been found in, weather conditions and the rangers' statements before leaving with the body. There was no way she'd be able to manage getting back up there a second time. The tiny life form growing in her uterus was already demanding a second breakfast and a nap and wanted her to throw up all at the same time.

Clutching the van's door handle, she tried to breathe through her nose. Crisp fall air helped with the permanent acid lodged in her throat but did little to ease the shock assaulting her every few thoughts. She could only imagine what her baby would think of all the embalming fluid and bodily fluids that made up her day when she got the body back to the office. Drennan swallowed a rush of nausea, slapping her hand against her mouth.

A baby. She was going to have a baby. There was no

denying the symptoms anymore. No trying to blame the flu or some other kind of illness.

"You okay?" The deep rumble of his voice soothed her stomach.

She'd recounted that voice so many times in the past two months. Imagined how it would sound whispering all the words she craved to hear. Not just from that night, but if they'd ever come into contact again. Drennan forced herself to face him.

Harvey. The name fit him. Rough around the edges, kind of like him, with a shadowed side and a fierce expression. His thick beard worked to hide his expression, but the deep tan he'd gained on the trails and the lines between his brows told her he much preferred to be outside than be cornered and forced to make conversation. He'd swiped his styled hair back away from his face. Not a hint of gray despite her guess putting him closer to forty than thirty. Then again, what did she really know about him other than the feel of his body pressed against hers, how it felt to have his mouth at her neck, his heightened breathing etched into her memory. He was even more handsome than she remembered. A mountain of muscle stretched against his ranger uniform. One wrong move would split the seams, and a flush of heat washed over Drennan at the random thought she'd pay good money to see that.

He'd said something. Right? Oh, hell. He was staring at her with nothing but expectation and disappointment—a look she'd come to know all too well—as if she'd grown two heads. Wait. Did she technically have two heads right now? No. It took more than eight weeks for the baby's head to develop. "What?"

"You look like you're going to throw up." Harvey offered a metallic water bottle. The black exterior was dented and scratched up. Used. His. "It doesn't take long for dehydration to set in, even in these cooler temperatures. It's all about exertion."

It wasn't until that moment that she realized how thirsty she really was. She took the offering, slugging back three huge mouthfuls of ice water. Streams escaped from the corners of her mouth. She swiped at her face with the back of her hand as embarrassment charged. Her mother's voice instantly scolded her to clean herself up. To stop acting like a child who couldn't control herself. Drennan practically shoved the water bottle into Harvey's chest as embarrassment overheated into shame. "Thanks. Do you usually offer your personal water bottle to anyone who feels like they might die out here?"

"Only the ones who've been in my bed." One corner of his mouth turned up, though it would've been impossible to catch with the amount of facial hair if she hadn't been looking right at him.

"Right. Listen. I'm sorry about before. Ambushing you like that. I'm sure the last person you expected to see today was one of the women you took home from a bar two months ago." Oh, no. Why did that make her sound so needy? He'd probably taken a half dozen women home since the night they'd shared. He probably didn't even recognize her. She wasn't anything special. To anybody. The ground went unstable under her feet. Only this time she couldn't contribute it to the pregnancy. She just wanted nothing more than to get in her too-hot van and shut herself inside the office with no plans to ever leave. Drennan took a deep breath and spun for the van's driver's side door. "You know what? It's been a long day, and you said you wanted to talk about this later. Now that you know who

I am, you can call the Metland Mortuary and ask for me when you're ready to talk."

Her hand was on the door handle. She was almost free of one of the most embarrassing moments of her life.

"The only woman." He didn't have to raise his voice for her to hear him over the traffic coming in and out of the visitor's center, as though her senses were intently tuned to him.

The breath rushed from her lungs as Drennan angled away from the van. He'd closed the distance between them, settling his hand against the driver's side window beside her head. Caging her. Not in intimidation or dominance but like he couldn't stand for a mere inch between them. "What?"

"You said one of the women I took home from the bar." His gaze locked with hers. Unwavering and confident. Just as strong as the night he'd caught her attention across a dark, crowded pub when she'd needed it most. "I don't make a habit of bringing women back to my place. You're the only one."

Okay. Why did that make her heart rate do a little dance in her chest? Drennan pressed her shoulders into the van for some added support, but it didn't do a damn bit of good. Because she'd learned real fast when this man infiltrated her personal space, physics no longer had a say. "Oh. Why?"

Instant regret hollowed through her. And then reflected in Harvey's expression. He added a couple of inches between them, removing his hand from beside her head. The cage was open, but she found herself missing it. Just as she'd missed it since backing out of his driveway two months ago without even knowing his name. She could've gone back. She remembered the exact location of his cookie-cutter house in the middle of a cookie-cutter neighborhood in Springdale, but that night… It'd been special. A once in a lifetime experience she didn't believe could be replicated or should be replaced with new memories. But if she hadn't sounded needy before, she certainly did now. "I mean, why me? Not that you couldn't or shouldn't take home whoever you want. From bars or the grocery store or work. You're handsome and attractive, and I bet you can get any woman you want if you put your mind to it."

Wide blue eyes narrowed on her, and the random thoughts in her head disappeared. "Take a breath, Drennan."

Her name on his lips shot something electric and addictive straight to her low belly, which she was sure was not his intention in the least. Her body seemed to obey his command all the same, and she drank in a full inhale, letting it out with an exaggerated sigh. What on earth had he seen in her that night he'd taken her home? She was a mess. And things were about to get much worse.

"Are you sure you're pregnant?" Harvey sounded so calm, her nerves automatically settled, which didn't make sense. This situation they were in was anything but calm. "You said you were on birth control."

The ego it'd taken to be one of the best emergency room physicians in the country wanted to take offense at that, but it was a valid question. She couldn't blame him for wanting confirmation. "The six tests I took seem convinced I am. Not to mention all the fun stuff coming out of my body."

"All right." He scanned her face from forehead to chin. Looking for the lie? Unfortunately for him, he wouldn't find one. "And you're positive the baby is mine?"

"You're the only…" She cleared her throat, focusing on the impossibly tall cliffs that seemed to blend right in with the clouds. Every second that body waited in the back of the van to be transported to Dr. Yarrow was another second the evidence could be compromised, but this… This felt more important. Like she was standing on the edge of one of those cliffs, and Harvey was the only one who could save her. She could fall alone, or he could pull her back. She had no idea what to do with a baby. She'd only taken a semester of obstetrics, and most of her work with pregnant mothers in the ER was referred to the maternity ward. She understood the basics of pregnancy and childbirth, of course. But what would happen after she took her baby home from the hospital?

Real fear simmered under her skin. How was she supposed to work and care for the baby at the same time? Where was the baby supposed to sleep in her one-bedroom apartment? What all did a baby need to survive? Would she and Harvey share custody or would he expect her to move in with him after she delivered? Question after question with no end in sight.

Sweat that had nothing to do with the midday temperature slicked the back of her neck. She…she couldn't do this on her own. "There isn't anyone else it could be."

Harvey slid both hands into his uniform slacks and broke his gaze off from hers. A hardness that hadn't been there a moment ago edged into his jaw. "Then what is it you want from me? Money?"

Her lips parted with an answer, but she didn't have one. Was that what he thought of her? That she'd told him for a payout? A sinking feeling crushed the last bit of nausea, intensifying the heaviness in her limbs, and she felt as though she really was standing on the edge of that cliff. Reaching for him and meeting nothing but air. And a small part of her that'd hoped for a different reaction—the part she'd clung to since seeing those two pink lines—died.

Her job as an assistant medical examiner didn't pay much—no government job did—but she'd been smart with her salary in her former life. She didn't need to work for a few years, but starting fresh here had meant using her skills and ridiculously expensive education for something new. Continuing to help people, providing answers and closure to the families she worked with. Drennan shook her head. "No. I just…thought you deserved to know. It's your baby, too. I think you should have a say in how he or she is raised."

Harvey scrubbed a hand down his face. "So you're keeping it?"

The thought of not seeing this pregnancy through hadn't even crossed her mind. From the moment she'd read that first pregnancy test—and the five after—she'd known her decision. There wasn't anything more important to Drennan than the family she'd had once upon a time—before everything had changed—and if there was even an ounce of the love she'd felt as a kid she could give to this child, she would do everything in her power to make it happen. A surge of defensiveness arced through her. "Yes."

"All right. I'll help. Clothes, college, braces, even your doctor appointments, I'll support him or her. If you want me to pay child support and have a lawyer draft up an agreement, I'll sign it, but I think I need to make something clear, Drennan. I'm not interested in being a father." Harvey stepped into her, close enough to touch, and lowered his voice before maneuvering around her to the front of the van and toward the visitor's center. "When it comes to raising this baby, you're on your own."

Chapter Four

He wanted to kick his own ass.

Harvey set sights on his SUV parked across the lot of the visitor's center and headed toward. His shift had ended nearly two hours ago, and he was working off less than a handful of hours of sleep. The estate lawyer just wouldn't give up. Calls, messages, voicemails, letters. He didn't want any of it.

He didn't want a damn thing from his father.

Every decision he'd made over the past twenty years had been in exact opposition to the son of a bitch who'd claimed to raise him, but even in death, his father was going out of his way to make Harvey's life hell. The military had given him an out, but twenty years hadn't provided nearly enough distance between them. Then the bastard had to go and die from a stroke and leave him everything. Life insurance policy, checking and savings accounts, the house… What had been going through his father's head when he'd signed his will and trust, Harvey didn't know. They hadn't talked in decades. Just how Harvey had liked it after everything that man had put him and his mom through. The abuse had killed her in the end. Not all at once, but a slow draining Harvey had never been able to put a stop to, and he wouldn't accept a penny or sign a single document admitting he was his father's son. No matter how many times the estate lawyer tried to convince him otherwise. Everything he'd done had been to ensure he never ended up like that man. Miserable. Angry. Strung out and blaming his problems on anyone but himself. Harvey wasn't going to be that person.

Except he'd just offered to financially support his and Drennan's kid. And while his biweekly National Park Service paycheck covered rent, food and transportation, it wouldn't stretch as far with a baby in the picture.

Hell. He could've handled her news better. Should've taken the time she'd offered for him to get his head straight. To explain. A baby. He was going to be a father whether he was involved or not, and the shot of terror he couldn't swallow since she'd given him the news doubled.

Harvey added more weight to his opposite leg, but there was nothing that would relieve that pain until he got off his feet, popped a few ibuprofen and iced his knee until his next shift tomorrow morning. Switching his water bottle from one hand to the other, he attempted to balance his weight, but it wouldn't do any good. Never did. The army had spit him out without an option to re-up thanks to the piece of shrapnel lodged under his kneecap, and he'd decided the best choice to prove them wrong was hiking up and down these cliffs all damn day. Seemed he had a knack for making stupid decisions.

Screeching tires peeled through the parking lot. He caught sight of the plain white van he'd helped load a body into skidding to a halt. The driver's side door shot open, and Harvey abandoned his escape.

Drennan scrambled from the driver's seat and doubled over, hands pressed against the van's panels as she heaved.

Harvey was already moving across the parking lot to-

ward her, a knot of something he didn't recognize squeezing his chest. Pain flooded from his knee into his upper
thigh as he picked up the pace, holding him back from an
all-out sprint to get to her. "Drennan?"

She flung a hand out. "I'm fine. Just stay back. You
don't… You don't want to see this."

Her hair fell over her shoulder as she heaved again. The
water she'd gulped after their descent from Emerald Pools
splashed across his boots. Harvey gathered her hair back
out of the way and set his free hand along her spine. His
stomach convulsed at the thought of her so miserable in
this heat. "Believe me, I've seen worse."

Her shallow exhales caused her back to arch against his
hand, and he started soothing circles into her skin. Nothing
but a distraction she needed to breathe through the nausea.
It helped sometimes. He'd seen enough soldiers lose their
breakfasts, lunches and dinners from the crap they'd had
to face overseas on the front lines in Afghanistan. Bodily
fluids hardly scared him.

Drennan swiped at her mouth but didn't move to
straighten. Waiting for the next wave? "You're right. Pulling a body from the pond this morning is worse. You win."

"I wasn't even thinking about that." He couldn't stop
the laugh escaping his chest. Even in the face of one of the
most uncomfortable situations, she managed to shift his
mood. But hadn't that been why he'd approached her in that
bar in the first place? She'd smiled at him from her single
table with a beer in hand, and all that rage and betrayal he'd
held on to since the funeral disappeared. Instant magic. It
hadn't taken much to convince himself to chase that feeling straight into his bed, and hell, she'd done an amazing
job in helping him pretend the world could stop turning.

"You've seen worse than a dead body?" Drennan shifted

away from the fluid inching into the cracks of the broken asphalt.

"I was military. Infantry. You see a lot of stuff you never thought you'd be able to stomach on the front lines." But he didn't want to think about any of that. "Are you sick, or is this…"

"Morning sickness?" She faced him then, tugging her hair free of his hand, a little paler than when he'd told her he wouldn't help her raise this baby a few minutes ago. Despite the circumstances, she couldn't even bother to look anything short of beautiful with all those sharp features, an inner glow and a few shards of hazel in her green eyes. Otherworldly and powerful as she'd been the night they'd met. She closed her eyes, her shoulders rising on a deep inhale. "Sure. You could say that. Except it's almost lunchtime, and the body I have stashed in the back of the van is starting to smell of algae and decomposition in this heat."

His cringe filtered into his expression. He didn't know a whole lot about pregnancy short of what his mother had told him of his birth story and the cravings she experienced while she was pregnant. Everything else in that arena he'd picked up in health class or by experimenting with girlfriends. His dad certainly hadn't given him any of those talks other than threats if Harvey had ever got a girl knocked up. Funny how the old man's death had led to just that. "Anything help?"

"Not that I've found." Swiping at her face with her sleeve, Drennan motioned to him. "Thanks for the assistance. My hair appreciates you keeping it vomit free."

"Anytime." The word had slipped out naturally, and Harvey instantly regretted the offer. He'd made it clear he'd support their child financially. Getting involved any further opened him up to a world of mistakes he wasn't looking to repeat. Ever.

Silence cut between them as Drennan seemed to weigh the slip. A good man who'd gotten a woman pregnant would want to know every symptom, every change she was going through to ensure her and the baby's health. He'd go out of his way to make things easier for her and go the extra mile to meet those midnight cravings. But Harvey wasn't a good man. He'd been corrupted the moment his dad's fist had first met his face, and he'd do whatever it took to protect Drennan and this baby from that future.

A horn blared from behind him. A car had rolled up a few feet short of the van, waiting for them to get out of the way.

Drennan practically jumped out of her skin, and reality rushed to meet them all over again. She hiked a thumb over her shoulder, stepping backward toward the driver's side door, and that sick feeling charged through him. "I better get going. Heat tends to speed up decomposition. Could alter the time of death readings and compromise any evidence."

He needed to let her go. To go home and ice his damn knee and recover enough for him to hike those trails all over again tomorrow. Except he was stepping into her all over again. "Give me your phone."

"What?" Those already wide eyes of hers grew impossibly brighter.

"Come on!" The car horn blasted a second time.

Harvey turned, holding up a single finger for them to wait. "Your phone."

Slipping the device free of her back pocket, she handed it off with shaky fingers. "I think they want my parking spot."

"I don't really give a damn what they want. You're more important than a parking spot." He made quick work of tapping the phones together. "Now you have my number. Message me when you get the bills from the doctor's office or if there's an emergency."

"Okay." She took her phone back—still shaking—and made it one more step toward the driver's seat. "How about now?"

His instincts fired in warning. Harvey countered her retreat. "Drennan?"

"I don't feel so good." She reached for him. Just before her eyes rolled back. She swayed on her feet as she had at the edge of the upper emerald pool.

Harvey caught her a split second before she hit the side of the van. Pain flared up his leg from her added weight. He couldn't stop the strength from giving out. His knee slammed into the asphalt, and they fell together. "Drennan."

"I'm okay." Her voice had gone breathy, barely audible over the grumble of the waiting car's engine, but she'd yet to open her eyes. "Just dizzy. I think... I think I need to lie down."

A car door slammed. Movement registered in his peripheral vision. The driver waiting for the damn parking spot. "Hey, man. Is she okay?"

"Help me get her in the passenger seat." Harvey did his best to get to his feet, but his knee had reached its limit. It took everything he had to trust the driver with the woman in his arms. A ridiculous notion considering he and Drennan weren't anything more than acquaintances, but possessiveness strangled him all the same. Together, he and the driver maneuvered Drennan into the van, but the vice around his rib cage refused to release until he'd climbed behind the wheel and tore out of the visitor's center parking lot.

Screw the body in the back. Something was wrong. Pregnant women didn't just pass out for no reason. He might not want to be part of this baby's life, but he'd sure as hell step up when it came to its well-being. He owed Drennan that much.

Pulling in front of the small Springdale emergency clinic, Harvey left the van running with air-conditioning to counter the heat collecting around the body in the back and rounded the hood to Drennan's side. His knee threatened to give out a second time, but he bit through the shredding discomfort, lifting her against his chest with an unfamiliar panic building behind his sternum. "Almost there."

The glass doors parted as he pushed himself to his limits. Two nurses caught sight of him and rushed to meet him halfway with a stretcher. Harvey laid her out, every sense he owned screaming to get her back in his arms. "She passed out about ten minutes ago after throwing up. She's pregnant, about eight weeks."

"We'll get her checked out as soon as we can." The nurse strapped a blood pressure cuff around Drennan's arm and pressed a stethoscope to her chest as the stretcher headed for the back rooms. Then cut her attention to Harvey. "Sir, you have to let go of her hand. Unless you're family, you're not permitted back here. Are you the father of the child?"

He hadn't realized he'd intertwined his hand with Drennan's and released his hold. Instant cold flooded through him at the loss of her warm skin pressed against his, but Harvey had survived this loss two months ago when he'd let her drive away. He'd do it again. For Drennan and the baby. "No. I'm not the father."

Chapter Five

Ugh. She hated that sound.

Drennan could feel the tug of the IV in the back of her hand. The slight cold burn of fluids eased through her veins before warming up in her forearm. Every sense she owned felt intensified, from the overly loud pulse of the heart rate monitor to her left and the shuffling and voices outside the curtain surrounding her bed to the air-conditioning blowing straight down on her.

A hospital. The unconscious haze cleared with deeper inhales. Familiar calls on the muted PA and scuffed tennis shoes hit that aching place inside of her that missed her former life. An ER—even on slow shifts—had never been boring.

The stained cream-colored curtain ripped to one side on metallic shower hooks, putting a thin dark-haired woman with a clipboard clutched to her chest swallowed by her white coat in Drennan's personal space. Rich brown eyes locked on her with a hardness that had no business on the doctor's face. "You don't call. You don't write. The first I hear about you taking that job with the ME is by your ass landing in my ER."

Drennan attempted to sit up, only to be humbled by the overwhelming sting in her hand from the IV line. Hospital.

Throwing up. Passing out. Her heart rate double-timing as panic took hold. "The baby—"

"Perfectly healthy. No issues that we could see." Dr. Cassidy Duffy navigated around to the side of Drennan's bed, checking her IV bag and the stats the machines picked up every few seconds. The woman exemplified the girl next door, with long brown hair, a soft smile that reached her eyes and an openness that calmed patients under her care into a coma. Her accent—straight from the streets of Boston—could do wonders in a crisis. "Seems you got a touch of dehydration, and by a touch, I mean you could've died out there. You're smarter than this, D. What the hell were you thinking?"

Okay. Scolding and that accent didn't go well together. In her former life, Drennan had been the one armed with criticism in her Ohio ER. Cassidy had been the one to follow. She sank deeper into the clumpy pillows that'd seen far more than she wanted to think about. Acid coated the inside of her mouth, and she reached for the glass of water positioned on the small bedside table. "I can't keep anything down, especially fluids."

"Ah." Lowering onto the rolling stool beside the bed, Cassidy lost the clipboard and leveraged both hands on her blue scrubs. Once one of Drennan's subordinates, she'd gotten out of Ohio to take the lead in her own ER, as small as it was. Cassidy had never explained the sudden move, but Drennan could probably relate more than most for the need to make drastic changes. "You see an ob-gyn yet?"

Drennan sipped at the water, not looking for a repeat performance of what'd happened in that parking lot. Definitely not her finest moment. "Just found out this morning. The constant throwing up was a good indicator. Well, that, and the missed periods. Got a recommendation?"

"Dr. Santori. She's on staff here at the clinic. I'll tell her to expect your call and you need an appointment, especially after what happened today. But for the next hour, we've got you hooked to electrolytes and fluids." Cassidy scanned her from head to toe then back, shaking her head. "So I take it the irritatingly handsome bulldozer demanding answers from my front desk staff is the father?"

Harvey? Fractures of memory filtered through the embarrassment doing its best to drown her in the middle of this mattress. Oh, hell. She'd never be able to face him after this. Passing out from simple dehydration? Her mother's voice was right there, incessant and needling. *What kind of doctor are you? Eight years of medical school didn't teach you you have to drink water to survive? How are you going to help other people when you can't even take care of yourself? Forget about—*

"Stop that." Cassidy's voice went from friendly to firm in a split second, and Drennan couldn't help but let appreciation chase back the darkness that'd started moving in. This was why Cassidy Duffy had made an excellent assistant emergency physician. Her ability to read people, to know exactly what her patient needed in the moment, had saved too many lives to count. "I know that look. She's not here, Drennan. You left her behind in Ohio for a reason."

Tears burned in her eyes. So stupid. She could blame the hormones, but she'd had this reaction every time she thought about the relationship she was supposed to have with her mother. How close they could've been. Only now it was worse. Because there were things she needed from her mother. Questions she needed answered from the one person who was supposed to be here for her during this time, who'd gone through all of this once before. Baby showers and registries, breastfeeding or formula advice,

visits from Ohio and hugs when it got to be too much—
she wouldn't get any of it.

Not from her mother. And not from the father of her
baby.

Her stomach convulsed, but there was nothing left to
throw up.

It wasn't supposed to happen this way.

She hadn't given a whole lot of thought into Harvey's
role in this pregnancy, but she hadn't expected him to not
want to be involved at all. Sure, he'd offered financial support, but she'd already told him she didn't need his money.
So, what? She had to do this completely alone? No discussion? She knew the research. Children raised in single-
parent homes could thrive as well as dual-parent homes. It
wasn't the structure of the family. It was the quality time
and love that determined the success of a child.

But she'd wanted more for her child. She'd wanted him
to be excited and to maybe give her a hug to calm the sheer
panic that'd followed her around all day. But, apparently,
she'd have to settle for him paying for this emergency
room visit.

"Your mother doesn't get to live in your head for free."
Cassidy's plain, long fingers swept Drennan's hair out of
her face and twisted the ends into curls on the pillow.
"Make her pay rent. Understand? You set the rules. You
decide how much influence she and everybody else has
in this new life you're starting."

Drennan didn't know what to say to that. As much as
she appreciated Cassidy's attempt to bolster the boundar-
ies she'd been working to construct since leaving home,
some things just couldn't be fixed so easily. A chasm
wasn't made in a single day. It eroded little by little—
forgotten birthdays, criticism about her weight, spewed

regret for having a daughter like her. Years of covert toxicity with sprinkles of genuine affection had trained her to be grateful for whatever affection she could get, and she just needed some of that warmth to help her through this. From anyone.

"Now tell me what's going on with you." Cassidy grabbed for the clipboard and ran an observing eye down the page. "You called me up for a recommendation letter for a job you're too qualified for, then you show up pregnant and unconscious in the middle of nowhere Utah three months later."

Drennan didn't have the energy to get into it, but Cassidy could quite possibly be the only friendly face she had in this new life. Dr. Yarrow hadn't batted an eye at her work history, and he was pleasant enough when things were going his way, but he was her boss. Nothing more. And Harvey… She didn't know where they stood. He'd gotten her to the emergency room in Springdale, but that had probably been more out of obligation to their child rather than genuine concern. The heaviness he carried in his expression hadn't been there the night they'd met. She didn't know anything about how it'd gotten there. Didn't know him other than he worked as a national park ranger and had once been in the military through his own admission, and while she couldn't even think about regretting this baby, she hadn't planned for this, either. They weren't friends. They were barely more than acquaintances, pulled in together on a case of drowning in the park. "It's a long story."

"All right. Another time then." The head of the ER leaned back on her stool before shoving to stand. Hints of soap and disinfectant tickled Drennan's nose as Cassidy leaned across the bed to detach the IV. "Well, you've had your required fluids and electrolytes. You know the drill. Little sips of water throughout the day. Eat calorie dense foods to get as much energy as possible. I can prescribe the anti-nausea meds if you think that will help with the vomiting, but Dr. Santori will want to follow up with you in the next day or two. That bulldozer out there going to take you home?"

"I'll call a rideshare." Oh, crap. Defeat drained the last of her reserves as she hovered on the edge of the bed. The van. She'd been on her way to the funeral home when her stomach had lost its ability to put up with the smell coming from the back cargo area. Drennan checked her smartwatch. Three hours. She'd been here for three hours. The heat would've severely altered the body's decomposition rate and any evidence that might've been left behind. She'd compromised a homicide investigation. "I have to go."

"Don't let me catch you in here again, D." Cassidy hugged her clipboard to her chest. "You take such good care of everyone else. I'll box your ears if you're not taking care of yourself."

"I don't know what that means, but I'll be careful." Her feet didn't feel like her own as she shuffled free of the curtain and headed for the front of the clinic. The bandage on the back of her hand itched like crazy, and she felt like a rhino was sitting on her bladder, but that was nothing compared to the shock of seeing Harvey pace back and forth across the waiting room. Her stomach dropped out, her throat going dry. A swell of heat had her grabbing for the nurses' station desk.

He'd waited for her.

That intense gaze that'd dragged her in like a strong pull of gravity that night at the bar settled on her. Harvey closed the distance between them. "You good?"

"I'm fine. To be fair, you warned me about dehydration out in the park. I guess with the death scene and the news, it slipped my mind more than usual." Was she fine, though? A strange twist of warmth knotted in her lower belly, and Drennan tightened her hold on the cold surface of the desk to keep herself from leaning into him to get more of it. She sucked in a sharp breath to contain herself. She pointed to the front doors. "You didn't have to wait. I planned on calling a rideshare."

"I wasn't just going to leave you here to deal with everything alone. They wouldn't let me in, though, since I'm not a relative." His hand shifted as though he might reach for her. Right where their baby was growing, but he pulled back, thinking better of the contact. Clearing his throat, Harvey straightened impossibly taller. "The baby?"

She…didn't know how to do this. The hot and cold back-and-forth. One minute he wanted nothing more than to keep his distance in every regard but financially, the next he'd admitted to his concern for her. Or was it just societal pressure and customs to make sure the woman you knocked up after a one-night stand was physically okay? Drennan couldn't read him as well as she could that night, and she hated it. The constant need to be on guard for the next threat to her mental health, the fact he felt the need to protect himself from her in the first place. "No problems."

"Good." He grabbed for her hand, rough calluses and another dose of that comforting heat scraping into her palm. "Then I'm taking you home."

Chapter Six

What the hell was wrong with him?

Harvey maneuvered his SUV into the driveway as carefully as possible, all too aware of the woman passed out against the window in the passenger seat. She'd fallen asleep almost the minute she'd settled in the vehicle. Exhausted and still recovering from this morning. He'd offered to drive her home, considering Dr. Yarrow had made a special trip out to collect the van with the body still strapped into the back, but the second he'd left the clinic parking lot, he'd dreaded waking her to ask for her address and headed straight to his house.

Drennan had been through a lot in the past few hours. Not only passing out from dehydration but having to make the climb and descent down the Emerald Pools trail while pregnant. Most hikers struggled with the incline on a good day, and she'd tackled it like a pro. Well, a pro who'd shown up strictly to do her job and hadn't considered she'd need a few hours' worth of water and calories.

He shoved the vehicle into Park, unable to help himself from studying the soft lines of her face in sleep. His brain had conjured a whole catalog of false situations and imaginations when it came to this woman. Not a single one of them had help up against the real thing. Drennan Hawes wasn't like anything he'd fantasized about. He didn't know a single person who would've kept as calm in her situation as she had. Most of the women he'd dated over the years had gone to the extremes to get his attention, to demand his concern, and yet Drennan had been more than ready to get herself home after being released from the clinic. Then again, she was a medical professional. He didn't know much about what it took or the education it required to become a medical examiner, but she was obviously levelheaded under pressure.

Where he'd nearly driven the nurses at the clinic to call security to remove him over his worry for her, she'd managed to bring him out of that spiral the second she'd walked into the lobby on her own two feet. How was that possible?

He was former military. Two decades of training had forced him to think logically instead of overreacting to any threat, but when Drennan had collapsed in that parking lot, every ounce of logic had died. He couldn't explain the sudden protectiveness that'd reared its ugly head. Just as he couldn't explain why he'd brought her back to his house. He and Drennan weren't a couple. They were barely acquaintances. Hell, he'd only learned her name a handful of hours ago, thrown together on an investigation he never wanted part of in the first place. But the tension in his chest wouldn't relent.

Shoving free of the SUV, he rounded to the passenger side, keys in hand. He popped her door and reached across her middle for her seat belt. His forearm brushed her low belly, right where their child was growing. Harvey froze, air crushing from his lungs, gaze locked on the soft rise and fall of her shoulders. No. Not theirs. Hers. Her child. He had no claim on the baby, and he didn't want it. He compressed the release for her seat belt, then threaded his arms behind her shoulders and at the backs of her knees.

His knee barked louder than ever before. One of the nurses had recognized him from a previous visit, noting the exaggerated limp as he carved a deep back-and-forth gorge through the lobby while the physician was tending to Drennan. In minutes, she'd arranged a cortisone shot to ease the inflammation, but the effect wouldn't take hold for a couple more hours. He'd survived worse injuries in his years growing up in his childhood home, and after everything she'd been through today, he wasn't going to ask Drennan to give anything more before she was ready.

A moan escaped her throat as he shifted her against his chest, her eyes fluttering against the sun's western assault. Her mouth parted on an exhale and reminded him of the few short hours she'd been tangled around him the night they'd met. How he'd played that exact sound over and over in his head, how she'd trusted him of all the people she could've gone home with in that bar. How she'd given him a gift of reprieve he'd have to work the rest of his life to repay. Starting now.

"Shhh." Harvey intensified his hold on her, that dark hole of all the things he'd imagined going wrong with her and the pregnancy calming as her body heat filtered through his uniform. She was here. She was alive. She and the baby were healthy despite what'd happened in the park. He hauled her up the three stairs leading to the front door and tapped in the key code for the smart lock, then kicked the door open. "I've got you."

She turned her face into his chest, as though seeking him out as they crossed the threshold. "Harvey."

An electrified shock shot straight from his head to his toes at the sound of his name coming from her lips. He'd been more than happy to go along with their silent agreement to leave everything they were out of his bedroom that first night he'd brought her home, to just be in the moment. But now, regret from not hearing her say his name on repeat as she'd shattered beneath his touch struck hard.

Using his heel to close the door behind him, Harvey headed straight for the back bedroom, bypassing his sad living room, the too-small galley kitchen and bare walls. Still carrying her in his arms. Where she belonged.

The thought brought him up short of crossing that second threshold. He stared at the crisp black comforter and sheets begging for her scent as much as his senses craved that dose of her in the weeks after she'd gone. Her lithe weight barely registered as an internal battle waged, though his knee had a bit more to say. Part of him recognized how easy it would be to settle her back in his bed. To allow her to claim it all over again, even just for a few hours of rest. Drennan would be comfortable and be able to sleep off the physical lethargy of the pregnancy, as she deserved. But that other part of him, the one that refused to drag her and the baby into the pain and suffering he couldn't stop carrying had him retreating back into the living room.

The couch wasn't new, the navy fabric stretching in some places and stained in others. A hand-me-down that served its purpose as a place to ice his knee and catch the next hockey game on his days off, but for the first time, he wanted to drive straight to the furniture store and buy something worthy of the woman in his arms. Something new with deep cushions, lots of space to relax or take a nap on and without stains. Maybe in her favorite color.

This whole house had come furnished apart from his mattress to serve as a low-rent option for rangers assigned to work Zion National Park. The one-bedroom, one-bathroom layout provided privacy without the need for a roommate and an escape when his people skills had run dry, which was more often than he wanted to admit. His lease kept him from painting the beige walls with a color from this century or from tearing up the peeling linoleum in the kitchen and the shag-like carpet through the rest of the place, but he'd managed to add some personal touches here and there. Though the stark realization of how little his child would enjoy a place so empty and bland shocked him straight to the core.

Damn it. Not his. He hadn't brought Drennan back here to play house. He wasn't going to have weekends with his kid or first steps in this room. The baby wasn't going to have a decorated room of their own or birthday parties at the kitchen table. This was nothing more than him ensuring the woman he'd gotten pregnant didn't pass out while behind the wheel on her way home. As soon as she was out of here, he'd go back to his pathetic life, his job that got him out of his head and keeping his distance from her.

Easing Drennan across the longest side of the L-shaped sectional, he untangled her fist from his uniform shirt and arranged a pillow behind her head. Dark eyelashes fanned across the tops of her cheeks, and he couldn't help but hold on to her hand a little longer as he realized how at ease she'd become despite barely knowing him. She needed to be more careful. Harvey smoothed a couple strands of hair away from her face, a jolt of want squeezing the air from his chest.

For quiet moments like this as they wound down from their jobs at the end of the day, for home-cooked meals spent right on this couch in front of the TV together. Probably burned if he was in charge of dinner. For breaking in this couch, the dining table, the kitchen counter, the hallway wall with their lovemaking, and filling this empty house with Drennan's gasps. For mornings when he could feel the baby kicking before she woke up and late night runs to the grocery store to fulfill her weird cravings.

His body moved without much conscious thought on his part. In this moment, Harvey could see it so clearly. Wanted it more than he'd wanted anything else in his life. He took a seat at the edge of the couch, careful not to rouse her, but Drennan turned into him, once again seeking him out.

But none of those wants were real. And they wouldn't ever be real. He was too corrupted by the evil that'd raised him to have anything so pure and beautiful to himself. Hadn't his father always warned him of that? That no matter how hard Harvey tried, he would always end up hurting the people he loved. He couldn't outrun it. That vicious streak for cruelty ran in his blood. Had become part of him from a young age. The betrayal, the rage. The military had helped him shape it into something useful, but now that he was a civilian, Harvey could feel it building up under his skin. Just waiting for the perfect opportunity to lash out. He would always crave to release the inner burn of anger in the most violent way possible, but he could do better than the men in his family had. He could make the choice not to let it ever touch Drennan or his baby.

The demon that resided inside of him—inside his father—would only be put off for so long. Mere days seemed to be the longest his dad could go without coming home from work wound too tight and ready to spring. On those nights, Harvey had managed to find someplace to hide for the most part, but he'd been too weak to protect his mother from taking the brunt of his father's anger. The bills they couldn't meet, too few work hours, his lack of promotion, spending money Mom didn't have permission to spend—it all combined into a hell Harvey hadn't been able to escape until he was eighteen. And in that hell an angel had suffered.

His mother's smiles had shone less as weeks and months and years under her husband's fists passed. The circles beneath her eyes had gotten darker. She'd gotten thinner. The most beautiful and kind woman he'd known had wilted to almost nothing by the time Harvey had been ten years old. It was why he'd never spent more than one night with a woman over the years, why he'd kept to himself in junior high and high school and throughout college and isolated himself from friends. No close relationships, even in the military, and he hadn't wanted them.

Until Drennan.

Harvey dropped his hand away from her face, forcing himself to stand and back away from the temptation sprawled across his couch. The hollowness that'd made him one of the army's finest infantrymen seemed to hiss at the loss of her skin pressed against his, but emotional—physical—distance was for the best.

He'd let her get some sleep, make sure she was eating enough for the benefit of the baby, then take her back to her place.

Stick with the plan, see it through.

It was the only way to protect her.

Chapter Seven

Her stomach groaned loud enough to wake her.

This was not her house.

Oh, crap. Had she passed out again?

Drennan shoved her upper body up, her elbows sinking into a sectional that'd seen much better days. Flickers of memory tried taking hold as she studied the simple living room. The layout looked familiar. A stinging in the back of her hand reminded her of the IV. Then Cassidy. And Harvey. He'd offered to drive her home, and then… She'd fallen asleep.

Collapsing back onto the mountain of pillows behind her, she stared at the swirling design in the popcorn ceiling. Harvey had brought her home. He'd carried her inside, set her up on the couch and covered her with what she could only imagine as the softest blanket she'd ever touched. Why? Why not take her straight home? Why go through all this effort for someone you had no intention of sticking around for?

Because he didn't know where she lived.

Right. Embarrassment at the slightest thought he'd gone out of his way for her out of affection flared.

You're nothing more than an obligation. You know that, right? He doesn't want you. It's that baby that's got him sticking around. Though I can't imagine why. Kids are nothing but a burden. Just like you.

Her teeth ached as she snapped her jaw shut. Her mother always seemed to have perfect timing when it came to reminding Drennan of who she was. Not the one people missed or the one someone worked to keep around. A passing thought, maybe. The one who took on the responsibility to check in with friends and go out of her way to ensure they had the support they needed. Never the one who was checked on. The only reason Harvey had brought her here was because she'd fallen asleep on the drive, and he hadn't wanted to wake her up.

Bits and pieces of the house's layout filtered into her memory from the one and only night she'd been here before. The hallway to her left housed a laundry closet. The doors had nearly buckled as Harvey had hauled her into them, his mouth insistent and desperate at her throat. Across from that, a small bathroom with a single vanity sink, toilet and shower stall where he'd disappeared to clean up then returned with a warm washcloth to help her do the same. Then the bedroom at the end of the hall. Where she'd lost herself in a man who'd looked at her as though she was the only woman in the world for him. Where she'd felt wanted and sexy and free for the first time in her life. No expectations. No promises. No disappointments.

She'd known her first one-night stand would change her life. She just hadn't expected it to change so much. She hadn't gotten the chance to tour the rest of the house, but she imagined the kitchen waited on the other side of the arch separating the living room from the rest of the house. All so different in the daylight.

Her stomach growled again. Somehow louder than before. Sitting upright, Drennan took a deep breath against the hunger pains threatening to eat her from the inside out. She slid her hand across her low abdomen, where she imagined the baby was having the time of its life with the concert her body was performing. "This is your fault. You won't let me keep anything down."

She scrubbed both hands down her face. She'd only found out she was pregnant this morning, and she was already talking to the ball of cells like they'd known each other for years. She needed to get out of here. The front door was right there. She could just leave. She could pretend she hadn't come face-to-face with the father of her baby at a crime scene and focus on the job she was meant to do. Though, she wasn't sure where her purse had ended up. Or her phone and keys. Oh, and the van with the dead body in the back. For crying out loud.

She grabbed for the blanket draped over her. It was worn, softer than expected for being knitted or crocheted—she didn't know the difference—and obviously well loved for years. Little bubbles of yarn caught between her fingers, laid out in boxlike patterns while the rest of the design seemed to frame each one in braids. The yarn itself had frayed in certain areas, especially at the edges, but there was something comforting about the muted gray color. Soft and warm and heavy. The afghan was like a giant security blanket specifically purposed to put her at ease. She hadn't noticed it the night Harvey had brought her home, but it was obvious from the scent of his body wash—something bright and earthy—he used it often.

"It was my mother's." His voice did something no amount of romance novels had accomplished, squeezing her insides until she was sure she'd snap from the tension. Harvey took position under the squared arch between the living room and where she imagined the dining room and kitchen waited. "Took her years to finish it, but once she did, she curled up with that thing with a book and tea in hand every day waiting for me to come home from school."

"It's beautiful." *Was his mother's. Did that mean she'd passed?* Her heart immediately jumped, wanting to find out as much as she could about the man who'd waited for her in the clinic lobby, but that little voice in the back of her head warned her off. Whatever this was between them, it wasn't more than responsibility. She had to remember that, but she didn't have to stick around to dig the knife deeper. Drennan couldn't help but give the blanket one more caress before she shoved to stand, straightening the imaginary wrinkles in her sweatshirt and jeans. Where were her shoes? "Well, thank you for allowing me to confiscate your couch, but I should get going. Dr. Yarrow has probably tried to get ahold of me a dozen times since this morning. I'm sure he's losing his mind wondering where that body is."

Oh, hell. The body. She could only imagine the damage done to the evidence in this heat. Hours of sped up decomposition could make or break this case, and she'd wasted nearly an entire day unconscious. Tears stung her eyes, but she wasn't going to let them get the best of her. At least not here where Harvey could hold it against her. She caught sight of her shoes and her purse near the door and made a point to focus on escape rather than the tendril of fear that grabbed hold at the thought of losing this job. It wouldn't be the end of the world with what she had in savings, but she genuinely needed this to work.

"I think he was more worried about you than the body." Harvey moved into the living room. And offered her a cup of pale-colored tea. Taking a sip from his own mug, he exuded calm when her entire nervous system threatened to throw her off the tracks. "I had some tea stashed in the cabinet from the last rangers who lived here. It's peppermint. I'm not sure if it's still good, but I read the caffeine in coffee increases the risks for miscarriage, leads to low birth weight and causes cognitive issues for the baby. And the peppermint is supposed to help with the nausea."

Her breath rushed out of her. Drennan wasn't sure if she was more caught off guard by the fact he'd spoken to Dr. Yarrow or that he'd read about the effects of caffeine on pregnancy. She took the mug, not entirely sure what to do next. Again, her stupid heart wanted to read more into his actions, but she shut that traitor up with a gulp of warm tea. The peppermint soothed the emptiness in her stomach, but she'd have to attempt to eat something soon to keep from passing out again. "You talked to my boss?"

Harvey stared at her over the top of his mug as he took another sip. He'd changed out of his uniform and into what she'd always thought of as lumberjack chic. The red-and-black-plaid button-down highlighted the thickness of his facial hair and intensified the blue in his eyes. His dark jeans carved out a very clear picture of how well he took care of himself as the muscles in his legs flexed with every shift in his weight while his boots held on to lines of crusted mud. Much like the night they'd met. He was a man who could lose himself in a national park, sit at ease in a crowded bar or hunt his own dinner. "Figured you'd need time to recover from what happened. Considering you've been passed out on my couch for the better part of three hours, I think it's safe to say I was right. I called him from the clinic. Told him to come pick up your van with the drowning victim in the back."

Holy hell. Her insides twisted in a way that had nothing to do with hurling her guts up. Drennan nearly choked on her next mouthful of tea. "Did you…did you tell him I'm pregnant?"

"No." Those dark, intense eyes held her prisoner as Harvey leaned against the archway guarding the rest of the house. "Wasn't sure if you were telling anyone."

She wasn't. At least, not until she'd wrapped her head around it first. Or maybe she was putting off telling anyone at all. Sooner or later, Dr. Yarrow would notice changes in her physical appearance. There wouldn't be any chance of hiding the pregnancy, but a piece of her wanted to keep the news to herself for a while. To have something that was solely hers, that no one could criticize her for. A ravenous flood of warmth assaulted her from head to toe that Harvey had made that same call she would've made on her behalf. "Thank you. For reaching out to him. You didn't have to do that."

She'd spent the better part of her life learning how to be alone despite having a living parent right there in front of her. But she wasn't alone anymore. And she wouldn't be for the rest of her life.

"Couldn't have you passing out on the way back to Hurricane and getting in an accident. Not sure your medical examiner could handle the influx in autopsies." His mouth twitched underneath all that beard. "I cooked up chicken and avocado quesadillas if you're hungry. From the sounds your stomach has been making, I'm guessing I'm not too far off the mark with that one, either."

Drennan waited for that all too familiar internal criticism laced with resentment, a lifetime of disappointment and failed dreams to cut through her. And waited. Her heart thudded hard in her throat. Seconds turned into a full minute, but the voice had gone quiet, and while the tension eased from her shoulders, confusion was making a comeback. "Why?"

His brows pinched together. "What do you mean?"

"A few hours ago, you made it clear you don't want anything to do with me or this baby other than paying child support." She fought against the urge to cross her arms over her chest, a surefire way to reveal the vulnerability she'd stopped letting people see a long time ago. "I mean why did you bring me back to your house? Why did you read up on caffeine and pregnancy, and why would you cook for me?"

Harvey didn't answer.

Maybe he didn't even know the answer, but Drennan had enough sense to recognize a one-sided effort when it was staring back at her. Yeah, it'd taken three decades to escape the one she'd left back in Ohio, but she was a much faster learner now. And a lot more self-aware of her part in letting people get away with disregarding her. She and Harvey were having a baby together, but the family she'd always wanted with the three kids and the house and the dog and the sickly-sweet passionate can't-keep-your-hands-off-each-other romance that should've come with it—those weren't realistic. Not for her, anyway.

"Why did you choose me that night?" It was the question that had rolled through her head every night when she stared up at her ceiling wishing for life to be different. For someone to want her as desperately as her dad had wanted her mom. And her heart hurt at the idea she'd never have it. Even with the father of her baby.

Harvey slid his hands into his pockets, every ounce the former soldier she imagined him to be. Brooding. Secretive. Heavy. "Because you were in as much pain as I was."

Chapter Eight

He could see it in her eyes.

The effort it took not to dart for the exit.

She didn't belong here in a crap-hole bar in the middle of nowhere. Harvey knew it. She knew it. The bartender throwing glances her way knew it. The sheer anxiety coming off her in waves pulsed every so often, a siren call he couldn't ignore. He was already two beers in, but he was clearheaded enough to take in everything about her, from the long fingers she curled around her own bottle to the slight bounce of her right leg on the stool. Long hair worked to escape the haphazard ponytail she'd attempted. Most likely in a rush. No hint of makeup, other than maybe around her eyes, or a whole lot of effort put into her outfit. Not meeting someone then. At least, not romantically.

He couldn't argue the jeans fit her like a glove, but the plain sweatshirt and tennis shoes did nothing to exaggerate her small frame. Like she'd gone out of her way to avoid garnering attention. Didn't help. He'd honed in on her the moment she'd stepped through the door. He hadn't noticed her in here before. So why in the world was a woman like her coming to a place like this?

Harvey wanted to find out. No. He needed to find out.

Her name, where she was from, where she'd gone to

school, if she was in town long—all of it. An invisible hook had snagged in his chest and refused to let up, itching and clawing and aggravating. Dragging his bottle across the soft, dented and scratched wood of the two-person table, Harvey navigated around a couple of regulars, barely dodging a collision with one of the waitresses who'd made it all too clear she got off around ten. He wasn't interested.

Heading straight for the bar, he clocked the patrons, their drinks, their moods and the exits. Couldn't stop himself. There were just some habits that refused to die after leaving the military. He hated that the training had been so ingrained it'd practically become part of him, eroding the man he'd been before he'd enlisted. Someone his mom might've been proud of. Couldn't say she'd be happy with him now, though. And maybe that was why he'd driven here straight after the funeral.

It wasn't often he felt the need to forget there was an entire world outside of these four alcohol and sweat-soaked walls, but he didn't want to remember today. Ever.

The woman's gaze—the greenest he'd ever seen—centered on him before he even had the chance to get close. As though she'd sensed him as much as he'd sensed her. Every move, every dart of her tongue across her bottom lip, every shaky inhale as she watched him approach. But more than anxiety resided in those eyes. Pain. A pain that called to his, matched his, maybe even outdid his. It blistered one second and healed over the next as though it'd never existed, but Harvey had more than enough experience to know it would never really die. Whatever had driven her to this bar wouldn't surface just once but a thousand times over. And some internal instinct told him she needed help outrunning it for the night. Anticipation widened her eyes, and he could've sworn she clutched her untouched beer a bit tighter.

Movement registered from his right and cut into his path. Broad shoulders blocked his view of her and pulled Harvey up short.

The man towered over her seat on the stool, leaning in. Hell, Harvey could smell the whiskey on him from three feet away. He'd been here a while, throwing them back with the two friends looking on from their table. College kids based on their baseball hats and hoodies, from over in St. George. "I've been watching you from over there. You all alone? You should join us."

Yep, that was the way to go. Intimidate the living crap out of her. Harvey couldn't stop the cringe from taking hold, and he tightened his hand on his beer much the same as she had a moment ago. He took up residence a couple stools down. Close enough to overhear, far enough away to pretend he wasn't interested in every word out of her mouth.

She swiveled in her chair, legs crossed, spine straight. Twisting the bottom of her bottle into the bar, she flicked her gaze to Harvey then to the man between them. Her shoulders deflated on a smooth exhale. "That depends. Are you the kind of guy that expects to me to laugh at your terrible jokes, pretend you're not thinking about getting in my pants the entire night and then let you send dirty pictures to your friends in the morning? Because I should warn you. I was raised to take care of my partner. Wash his clothes, clean the house, wear gloves, get rid of the body and act very sad at the funeral."

Harvey couldn't hold in the laugh caught in his throat but saved it with a cough. Or six. He tried taking another *drink, catching the kid's attention from over one shoulder, and waved the bartender off.*

"Forget you." The kid shoved off the bar, taking two wobbly steps backward, providing Harvey with another uninterrupted view of his current obsession. "You're like my mom's age, anyway."

She raised her beer in mock salute and took a drink. "I'm sure that sock by your bed will be happy to hear it."

The flash of despair was back, though she made sure to cut her attention back to the bar. But Harvey had seen it. He couldn't seem to look away. Holding his breath for the next moment that darkness reached out to him.

He turned to face her, never more patient in his life for her to look at him. And when she raised that green gaze to his, the confusion and rage circling in his head vanished. As though it'd never existed. He closed the distance between them, his beer forgotten on the bar. Not a single word spoken between them as he offered her his hand and nodded toward the door. It wasn't needed. Because whatever connection that'd drawn him in gripped her, too. Understanding on a cellular level he couldn't explain.

With a smile, she slid her hand into his.

"I don't know what pain you're talking about." Drennan cast her gaze around his bland house, anywhere but on him.

It was that same sense of anxiety he picked up on in the bar. As though her skin crawled with a thousand shards of glass. He understood that feeling, the need to escape. He shouldn't have approached her that night and saved her from his proximity altogether, but once she'd so creatively turned down that college kid's offer, he'd been snared. "You're good at hiding it. I'll give you that. One moment it's there in your eyes, then gone the next. Like your brain is recalling whatever happened over and over to keep you safe, and you're trying to live your life separate from it."

Her mouth parted, and Harvey had the distinct feeling he'd hit a nerve. He'd surprised her. Good. It was only fair considering the news she'd given him in the middle of a crime scene this morning. "You never actually drank your beer that night. In the bar. You kept picking at the label like you hoped someone would come along and take it away and tell you to get out. You didn't actually want to be there. I don't think you were hoping anything would happen. You just had nowhere else to go."

"You were watching me." She leveled her chin parallel to the floor in a show of confidence, but he couldn't help but watch the hint of pink slip up her neck and into her face.

"Kind of hard not to with the way your leg was bouncing off that stool." When had he stepped close enough to catch that addictive scent of hers? His entire nervous system latched on to the barest hint and settled a split second later. "The entire building was threatening to come down if I didn't distract you."

"Is that what you were doing when you came over?" Her voice turned breathy, as though just now recognizing the mere inches between them. "Trying to distract me?"

He angled his head to one side, heart rate climbing every second he stood his ground. "I'll admit I wasn't expecting the death threat you delivered to that kid, but I can't say I wasn't a little curious if you had one saved up for me that night."

"I might have." The humor drained from her expression, and the darker shift was back in her eyes. "But judging by the two bottles you had on your sad little table in the back corner, you were there to pretend reality didn't exist for as long as possible as much as I was."

He…hadn't expected that. Cold doused him from the inside out, and Harvey added that much needed space between them. Threading his hands through his hair, he let a low-key laugh escape his chest. Hell, she'd hooked him all over again. Dragging him in little by little with that gravitational pull that had caught him in the bar. And look where it'd led them. "Everyone needs a break from reality once in a while."

"You said you felt I was in as much pain as you were." Her accusation didn't come with pity. Just a simple request to understand what had brought them to this moment. They'd gone all night without saying more than a few requisite words to each other, using one another to escape hard truths and shattered expectations, and while he didn't owe her anything—they didn't owe each other anything— he could give her this. He could give her some insight into the man she'd tied herself to for the next nineteen years.

"The day we met, I'd just come from my father's funeral." He hadn't told anyone but his supervisor, and that had only been to get the day to drive north and back once the service ended. He'd been the only one to show at the small local church that'd hosted, and hell, wasn't that saying everything about his and his dad's relationship. There'd been nothing between them for the past twenty years, but Harvey just couldn't seem to let go.

Her expression shifted into sympathy. "I'm sorry."

"Don't be." He shook his head, adding another step between them as though his mere proximity would corrupt her. "He wasn't anyone to lose sleep over. Certainly not a man who deserves your sympathies. He was an abusive bastard who ruined lives, and I'm glad he's not able to hurt anyone else."

Drennan nodded in understanding, that intense green gaze fully locked on him as it had been that night he'd brought her home. Not a single ounce of judgment or criticism aimed in his direction. "But you went to his funeral."

"I needed to see him in the ground. I needed to make sure he got what he deserved." He'd never said the words out loud before, and that all too familiar growl of anger resonated through his chest. Nearing out of control. "I enlisted the second I turned eighteen. It was my way out, but that meant leaving my mom behind. I think she understood. She wanted me to get out, but six months into my first tour, I got the news she died. Scans showed evidence of chronic traumatic encephalopathy."

"Permanent brain damage from too many concussions." Drennan latched on to his forearm, squeezing it to provide comfort. She was a medical professional. It was in her nature, but all it did was remind him of the times his mom had tried to reach his dad in those late-night fits of yelling matches. And ended up paying the price. "Harvey, I'm so sorry. I'm sure your dad's funeral was hard no matter what your relationship with him entailed, but what happened to your mom is not your fault."

He wanted to believe her. Wanted to take her words and use them to drown the guilt and grief and rage until it couldn't get hold of him again. If anyone could help him forget the mess in his head, it was her. That invisible hook that'd snared him the night they'd met pulled taught, urging him to see the good she saw in him. But the demon in his blood wouldn't let him.

"I don't blame myself for my mother's death, but you need to understand something, Drennan." He stared at her hand, every cell in his body on fire, and backed out of her reach. Her face fell, stabbing the ache in his chest deeper. "My grandfather was an abuser. My father was an abuser, and I can feel it in me, too. This pent-up darkness just waiting to get out. It's what made me such a good soldier. Their legacy is in my blood."

She took a step back. Good. She should be scared of him.

"So you need to go home. You and the baby need to stay away as far from me as possible. I'll keep my word. I'll pay child support or whatever you need to raise him or her." It took everything he had not to promise he would be better than the men in his family. That she was safe with him. Harvey shook his head, keeping himself in the moment. Here, with her. "But as long as I'm in your or this baby's lives, I'm a danger to you."

Chapter Nine

She'd learned to walk on eggshells.

She'd learned to recognize certain footsteps, tones. How to tell if her mother was in a bad mood and when to avoid her. Drennan had learned to study people at a young age and could read almost everyone like a book before they spoke.

It was a trauma response.

Medical school had taught her that much. Hyperfocusing on what people said or thought was how she'd stayed safe in her unpredictable environment. At least, according to the psychology professors who'd required each and every student to participate in therapy sessions during the term focused on the mental health of future patients. Every shift in mood or behavior hit her upside the head because she was the one who would face the consequences of those shifts. She'd become habituated to the high levels of stress since her father's death. The result? She'd been a "good" girl. Praised for not having big feelings, not making messes, not making noise.

Until the pressure of being that good girl had torn her apart from the inside. Drennan forced herself to take a slow breath. Observation was still hard. Being watched. Noticed. It'd become a precursor to punishment once upon

a time, but the way Harvey had looked at her that night...
It was the same way he was looking at her now. As though
he'd been broken into a thousand shards of himself, begging for someone to come along and put him back together.
He was right before when he'd said her pain had called to
his. The same thing had happened in her chest. Latched on
to him and refused to let go. In that moment, she'd wanted
to be that person for him. To be the one to piece him back
together. Just as she'd treated and mended so many others.

Drennan took a step into him. Invading his personal
space. His shoulders tensed, his body preparing for the
threat his brain was trying to convince him existed. A
feral animal backed into a corner. One wrong move and
he'd lash out, but she wasn't scared of him or of anything
he'd told her about his family history. It was true a corre-
lation existed between living through abuse and becoming
an abuser. An entire third of children continued the cycle
and patterns of neglect and abuse brought down on them
through their childhoods, but Harvey wasn't ever going
to hurt her. Not like that.

Because that same part of her that recognized the shared
pain he'd talked about also recognized his pure need. He
probably didn't even realize how he'd held her a bit tighter
that night, how he'd sought her out in the dark as though
he couldn't stand to be parted from her, how he'd trusted
her and himself to get close. And she was going to prove
he wasn't anything like the parent that had taken the last
shreds of his worth. "Do you want to hurt me, Harvey?"

Surprise relaxed the muscles around his mouth and
eyes, and he seemed to draw his own deep breath. Clari-
fying. Cleansing. His gaze snapped to hers. "No."

She took another step, her chest brushing against the
hard planes of muscle beneath his shirt. Her pulse thudded

hard at the base of her throat to the point she thought he might actually be able to hear it. How could he not? According to him, she was putting herself at risk just being near him, but Harvey had gone out of his way to take care of her—to take care of this baby—since the moment he'd learned her name. "How about now? Do you want to hurt me now?"

The struggle to back off and put as much distance between them as he could manage flared in the flexed tendons of his neck and forearms. If she wasn't a medical professional, she might think the tension hurt as it tried to break free of his skin. His chest rose on a strong inhale, and he closed his eyes. Still fighting. "No."

"Do you see me as a threat, Harvey?" She wasn't a psychologist or a social worker. She had no business testing his limits without putting protections in place for herself, but whether Harvey trusted himself around her and the baby or not, she wasn't going anywhere.

He shook his head, as though not about to trust himself to speak, but still refused to look at her.

Drennan reached out, watching her fingers slowly slide up his forearm. Feeling the tendons beneath his skin. Dark hair parted under her touch, followed by a row of raised goose bumps. She ran her hand farther up his arm, across his shoulder, framed the side of his neck. Not a single inch of space separated them now, his shallow breaths skimming her jaw. A deep jolt of heat speared through her nervous system as she caught another dose of that earthy scent she'd associated with him since the night they'd met. "Do you know why men like your father feel the need to overpower those weaker than them?"

Harvey didn't move, didn't even seem to breathe now.

"They manipulate, control, dominate and destroy anything and anyone that makes them feel because they're not emotionally mature enough to cope with the people in their lives and their surroundings. Their emotions and opinions weren't welcome or important growing up, and so they found a way to make themselves important. Heard, even. They suppress everything until all that's left to break through is anger, outrage and stress. They let themselves be overrun by it minute to minute and end up taking out that immaturity on the people they're supposed to love." Her voice threatened to lodge in her throat on that last word. Tears sprang in her eyes as her attempt to get through to Harvey hit too close to home. Always the mediator, always the one who needed to fix things so she wouldn't be punished. So she would be seen by the one parent she had left. It didn't do any good. It never changed a damn thing, but she could help him. Right here in the middle of his living room, she could make him see the truth. Drennan leaned in, her mouth brushing at the corner of his. His beard pricked at her skin, sending a shock of sensation through the rest of her. She set her free hand beneath his opposite wrist and tugged his fingers to her hip, then did the same with his other hand. "I trust you not to hurt me."

Harvey's eyes snapped opened, brilliantly blue and as compelling as she remembered. He took an initial step back, but Drennan only tightened her hold on his hands at her hips. "You shouldn't."

Gravel coated those two simple words, and her heart broke a little more for him. For what he must've been through as a child, for the darkness he surely carried having to leave his mother behind to escape, for the pure self-loathing that simmered beneath every word out of his mouth.

"I trust you because you offered me your hand that night

at the bar." She pressed a kiss to the side of his mouth, instantly lost to the feel of a warm-blooded man who'd wanted her. Who didn't see her as anything like a tool to be used or someone to exert power over. "You gave me a choice."

She swept her bottom lip across his, countering his step to escape, and kissed the opposite side of his mouth. He opened to her slightly, his breath mingling with hers until she wasn't sure where she began and he ended. "You brought me to a place you feel safe. You touched me with nothing but respect and followed my every cue. You let me take control of the situation as though you were simply grateful I was there. So no matter what you might think of yourself, I know you're not like him or your grandfather or anyone else who has used their power to diminish someone else's."

One second. Two. She'd made her point, and despite the unfiltered desire heating her blood, Drennan moved to step back. To give him the space he obviously needed. Once again, he'd swooped in to save her, to take care of her, but this was the kind of man who would never see himself as any kind of hero. And she would leave if that was what he required.

But his hands tightened on her hips, holding her hostage.

Her adrenaline spiked for a moment, and she forcibly had to remind herself of everything she'd just tried to prove to him. She wasn't scared of him. If anything, she wanted more, and that scared her more than anything. Her desperation for him to want her, to choose her when no one else had.

"Who hurt you?" The gravel hadn't left his voice, and

with the descent of the sun coming through the front window, she couldn't be sure of his expression.

This wasn't about her, and that ingrained urge to downplay everything she'd been through—because there were people out there, like him, who'd been through so much worse—reared its ugly little head. But she'd left Ohio for a reason. She'd seen the signs and sworn never to justify them again. Never to overlook the hurt and disregard, the neglect—any of it again. Drennan pressed her fingertips into the backs of his knuckles, steadying herself. But that didn't mean she had to expose that leaking wound. She'd moved on. She'd started a new life with a new job, a new apartment and a new outlook on life. And she wouldn't ever put herself in a position to be that victim again. Not even for him. She shook her head with a tight smile pulling at her mouth.

Harvey used both hands on her hips to back her against the arch separating the living room from the kitchen and dining room beyond. The corners dug between her shoulder blades with the weight of his body pressed against hers. Not to control or intimidate but something just as dangerous if she wasn't careful. Angling his head to one side, he skimmed his nose along her jaw, near the sensitive spot beneath her ear and down the side of her throat. Hovering over her pulse. "Do you know what I did in the military? What made me such a good soldier?"

She couldn't even shake her head, too lost in the full dose of heat sinking through their clothing. It was the same illogical reaction that had convinced her to go home with a practical stranger, bypassing every warning she'd been taught in school. Her fingers fisted in his shirt, to add much-needed space between them or draw him closer, she wasn't sure.

"I was an interrogator." His mouth slid to all the places his nose had visited, eliciting an eruption of desire in her low belly. "I could read people better than most. Tell when they're lying."

The muscles down her spine tightened one by one. A defense he'd definitely noticed given the hitch of his mouth into a smile against her skin. "And did you have to get this close to them to be able to tell they were lying?"

"No." Harvey slid his thumbs from her hips, to the hem of her sweatshirt then up. Calluses scraped against the bare skin of her stomach in small circles, working to ease the panic closing in around her throat. "Being this close to you when all I've thought about for the past two months is tracking you down and re-creating that night is just an added benefit. Who hurt you, Drennan?"

He'd wanted to find her? Drennan couldn't get her head around that. She shook her head, trying to convince herself more than anyone else. "It doesn't matter." It didn't. She wasn't a victim anymore. She didn't have to—

"You should know I have other ways of getting to the truth." A growl reverberated through his chest and straight into hers. He pulled back slightly, and the cold rushed in. His gaze dipped to her mouth then back. "And I'm very good at my job."

Harvey crushed his mouth to hers.

Chapter Ten

He hadn't meant to kiss her.

But Harvey pulled her toward him, dropped his head and lost himself in that near-constant craving he'd had for her since the night they'd met. Deeper, harder, more ferociously. His mouth smoothed over Drennan's as she met him stroke for stroke, like a dance they'd rehearsed a thousand times. In a matter of seconds, his entire body felt as though he'd been stunned with a Taser. His heart thudded hard enough from behind his rib cage, he was sure Drennan could feel it trying to escape.

His senses rocketed into overwhelming territory. Every sweep of his tongue against hers. He couldn't fight the urge to savor everything he'd convinced himself hadn't been real all over again. The slight gasp as he let up, the way her fingernails dug into his shoulders. How she pressed against him as though unconsciously seeking him out. His hands and legs prickled with sensation. Heavy as he folded her against him.

This. This was what he'd been missing the past eight weeks. Her touch, her scent, the way her hair slid between his fingers. Sex had always been nothing more than a biological necessity he was happy to get through, but with

Drennan… How had his brain minimized this connection between them?

Harvey slid his hands down, over her back end, down to her thighs and lifted her off the floor, securing her legs around his waist. Turning, he pressed her back into the archway. To get closer. To neutralize this need for her he thought might not ever be satiated. Years of numbness and avoidance broke under the small moan escaping up her throat. And Harvey wanted to hear it again. He wanted to hear it every morning and every night. Every time he touched her. It belonged to him, that sweet little sound. She'd never make it for any other man. She was his. Right here, right now. Whatever this was between them just made sense. The ache in his chest—where a hole had been for years—matched the one building through the rest of his body as he pressed into her. Only she could soothe it. Just as she had that night.

The night she'd gotten pregnant.

Blood drained from his upper body, too many sensations assaulting him all at once. His baby. She was having his baby. He was going to be a dad. And that…that couldn't happen. Right?

Pressing his forehead to hers, Harvey broke the kiss, breathing heavy. Her, too. He'd done that to her. Brought out that woman who'd shot down a college kid trying to get lucky, the one who'd taken his hand without a moment's hesitation and somehow shattered everything he'd ever known about himself in a single night. He wrapped her in both arms, holding on to her with everything he had. He wanted her. More than he'd ever allowed himself to admit to wanting something before.

She squeezed her thighs around him as his thumb traced the waistline of her jeans. Trying to drag him out of his head and back to her. Drennan arched her back to close the distance between them once more. "Harvey."

That breathy sigh nearly did him in. She skimmed her fingers over his jaw, turning his gaze to her. "Hey. Are you okay?"

It would be easy to haul her back into his bed, to chase that high she was solely responsible for addicting him to, but he'd always want more. Do whatever it took for the next hit, maybe even override her desires. And that… He wasn't that man. He wouldn't let himself be that man. Harvey loosened his hold around her rib cage, all too aware of how little pressure it would take to keep her for himself. "I can't. I can't do this."

She unlocked her ankles, sliding down the front of his body with both hands on his shoulders for balance. Lips swollen with the evidence of their kiss, Drennan ran a hand through her hair, still so close he could feel the gallop of her heart rate. "You realize we've done this before, right?"

He fought the laugh charging up his throat. Harvey pressed his hand into the archway at her back and shoved off. "Yeah. I'm aware, but this isn't happening. Not again."

"*You* kissed *me*." Her expression fell along with the volume of her voice. Almost as though she'd severed some innate part of herself from her emotions. From feeling anything at all. But Drennan was too alive for that, too beautiful for that.

And he hated it more than anything. He hated that she felt the need to protect herself from him, like he was a threat. But that was what he'd warned her about. That a switch he couldn't see inside could be flipped at any moment. That he could lose control and she would be the one to pay the price. He'd witnessed that same reaction from his mother too many times to count, that desperation to emotionally—sometimes physically—protect herself from his father. To detach. Which only added to his belief someone had hurt Drennan. No matter how much he wanted to push for answers—to have a name to put to the pain he caught in her gaze every once in a while—he wouldn't force her hand. He wouldn't add to her misery. Harvey backed up a few steps. "I made a mistake."

"You're not him, Harvey." She gripped the ends of her sweatshirt in both palms, seemingly unsure what to do with her hands, but not out of nervousness. "And I'm not a mistake. I'm a choice standing right in front of you. One you can make without the influence of the person who hurt you. I understand that sounds easier said than done, but it can be done. I'm proof of that. We're going to have a baby together. Isn't that worth something?"

He couldn't stop the flinch tensing his entire body. No. She wasn't a mistake. She was everything he'd ever dreamed about. And he couldn't have her. Not without breaking her as thoroughly as his mother had been broken. She deserved better than that.

"That's the thing." Heat that had nothing to do with the remnants of her taste on his tongue seared through his chest as he backed up another step. Wrong. This entire conversation on his end felt wrong, but he couldn't stop. For her. For the baby. He had to see this through. "You don't know me. I'm just some guy you met in a bar. You have no idea what I'm capable of."

"I thought I did, but you're right. How much do we really know about each other?" Her throat worked on a deep swallow, and Drennan darted her gaze to her things by the door before heading for them. He thought he'd seen a hint of silver lining her eyes, but it was gone before she turned back to face him. She grabbed for her purse, checking her phone briefly before shoving it into her bag. "It's been a long day, and I'm tired. Thank you for getting me to the clinic and letting me recover here. I'm going to call a ride-share and go home."

A hit of surprise nearly knocked him off his feet. She was leaving? Of course, she was leaving. He'd given her every reason to walk right out that door with the intention of letting her. He wouldn't stop her, but that deranged part of him that had been searching for her the past eight weeks wasn't ready to let go. "I can give you a ride."

Drennan slung her bag to one shoulder, and a wave of exhaustion played across not just her face but down her entire body. "Why, Harvey? Because you feel obligated to make sure the woman you got pregnant makes it home or because you want to give me a ride?"

He didn't have an answer for that. At least, not one that would convince her he wasn't completely out of his mind.

"You asked me who hurt me." She gripped the strap of her purse hard enough for the whites of her knuckles to show through the delicate skin on the backs of her hands. "There are people in this world who pride themselves on never putting their hands on someone who doesn't deserve it while tearing their victims down any way they can. Sometimes it's by making promises they never intend to follow through with or building up hope while intentionally planning on how to use their victim's weaknesses against them. They belittle, they lie, they exaggerate and turn your words back on you. Over and over until you're convinced you're the bad guy and they're the victim, but the worse part? You still want a relationship with that person. Because, in your mind, one glimpse at the good instantly outweighs all the bad. You want those moments where you matter to be true more than anything in the world."

Every muscle down his spine tightened under battle-ready tension. And he instinctually knew Drennan was speaking from experience, that someone had strategically torn her apart piece by piece. Preyed on her affections and used her vulnerabilities against her. It was an invisible kind of abuse that no one noticed—psychological warfare—and he'd... Oh, hell. He'd gotten her hopes up with that kiss.

"You said you didn't want anything to do with this baby. You don't think you're fit enough to be a father, and I will believe you if that's what you want. I will support your decision, and I will never hold it against you." Drennan shifted her bag farther up her shoulder.

The sincerity in that simple statement nearly crushed him. His choices had never mattered. Not as a kid and sure as hell not in the military. There was always someone overriding his free will and making decisions for him. From what he ate, to how long he slept, to where he was allowed to go and when. The only real freedom he'd experienced in the past few years was in the middle of nowhere trying to keep hikers from doing dumb things. Like get themselves killed. But Drennan... She'd just accepted him as if his decision mattered. Like he mattered. How? How was it possible that of all the people he'd been with over the years, this woman had the one thing he'd craved for years but was the one person he couldn't let himself have?

"What I won't do is let you play with my emotions or use me to test the limits you've set for yourself." Her shoulders rose on a strong inhale as she reached for the front door. "I've just stopped being an easy target for someone else. I won't be one for you."

Harvey didn't know what to say to that, what to think. He wanted to know who. Who had dared to convince Drennan she was anything less than the capable, optimistic, indispensable woman standing in front of him? A former boyfriend? A husband? "Drennan."

He wasn't sure if he was trying to stop her from leaving or if he just needed to say her name, to have it etched deeper in order to hold on to her a bit longer. Because she was going to walk out that door, and once she did, every ounce of training he had told him she wasn't coming back. That while he'd drawn the line between them, she would uphold it better than he ever could.

Swinging the front door open, she kept her hand on the knob, barely angling her chin over her shoulder, as if she couldn't even stand to look at him. And he deserved that. Hell, he deserved worse, and he would take anything she threw at him. "I don't need your financial support for the baby, Harvey. I was just hoping for you."

She stepped out into the night, closing the door behind her.

Chapter Eleven

Something oily took up residence in her veins.

Vulnerability felt like that. Thick and uncomfortable. Crap. She'd basically told Harvey that she'd wanted to be a couple before she'd escaped his house last night. To try to make this work between them.

Drennan was furious with herself for letting that buried little secret slip. She knew better. How many times had she voiced her wants and had them thrown back in her face or used against her over the years? She'd promised herself she wouldn't do this again, and she couldn't breathe through the tightness in her chest because of it. Embarrassment didn't cover it. This was outright fear. Conditioned into her over years of being told nobody in their right mind would choose her. That she was—

"No." Her voice echoed through the basement exam room, harsher than she'd expected. That voice didn't get to live rent-free. Like Cassidy had said. Drennan closed her eyes, setting her hands against the cold stainless steel of the exam table.

But that kiss… It'd held the kind of passion she'd always wanted. The desperate, hot kind that made her feel wanted and important. And while more than one night together hadn't been the agreement, she and Harvey really hadn't planned for a baby. That changed things, didn't it?

"Did you say something?" Dr. Yarrow entered their dark little exam room as she imagined someone might enter a formal event, all smooth lines, pressed seams and straight posture. Even his forehead didn't dare wrinkle despite his age being somewhere in the mid-sixties. The lab coat protecting his slacks and button-down hung off his shoulders with a little extra give down the sides. The man had single-handedly led the Office of the Medical Examiner here in Hurricane for over thirty years. With more natural deaths than homicides between the locals, Zion National Park and Springdale, there'd been plenty of time to take care of his physical health, but the stress around his eyes was starting to show.

"No. Sorry." Drennan got back to arranging the tools the ME would need to start the autopsy of the drowned victim from the park, everything from the bone saw to specimen tubes to collect bodily fluid samples as they progressed through their established routine. Thankfully, it seemed Harvey had acted quickly enough to call Dr. Yarrow to collect the body from the clinic parking lot that not a whole lot of damage had been inflicted on the remains by the extreme heat. She wasn't going to lose her job. Yet. "Just talking to myself."

"Must've been a hell of a conversation for me to hear it down the hall." Dr. Yarrow rounded the exam table and folded down the thin sheet providing a small modicum of privacy to their patient.

The victim had been stripped of her personal items, including her hiking gear, the beanie she'd been found in, her jacket, shirt, underwear, boots and socks. Impeccably arched eyebrows framed almond-shaped eyes, the deepest shade of brown Drennan had ever come across. Full lips, a blade of a nose, clear skin and healthy mid-back-length dark hair spoke of someone who took the time to take care of herself. Her body was soft, revealing the victim's preference for cardio rather than strength training. The blisters on the bottoms of her feet and the lack of wear on the hiking boots said this woman hadn't been much of an outdoorswoman or she'd started a new interest.

There hadn't been reports of any missing women as far as Drennan had been able to find when she'd contacted Springdale PD and Zion's law enforcement division head she'd met at the scene, but that didn't mean someone out there wasn't missing her or simply hadn't known where she'd gone. Drennan made a mental note to check in with the surrounding police departments. The victim was potentially young enough to fit in with the college crowd from St. George. Maybe someone had inquired after her there. Still, they had very little to go off of when it came to uncovering her identity. No driver's license or other form of ID had been discovered on the remains or in her backpack. It would take DNA, fingerprints or dentals to solve that puzzle unless the rangers could recover her missing personal items.

Dr. Yarrow tipped the victim's head back, unlocking her jaw to peer inside the woman's mouth before stepping back and donning his protective eyewear, gloves and mask from the secondary table she'd arranged while trapped inside her own head. "Are you feeling better today?"

Drennan nearly dropped the syringe she'd been in the process of handing off to collect fluid from behind the victim's cornea. Vitreous humor. It was just one of many samples they'd preserve for toxicology and reexamination down the line. She managed to hand off the syringe without losing the rest of her dignity. "Um, yes. Thank you."

"That park ranger—what's his name, Knight?—said you'd collapsed from dehydration." Strapping the magnifying glasses over his head, the medical examiner positioned the tip of the needle to the side of the victim's eye and pushed forward, pulling on the plunger at the same time. A filmy white fluid filled the syringe.

Drennan tried not to roll his name around in her brain for too long, but the unsolicited reaction started in her toes and tightened the skin on her scalp. Images of that kiss, of the way he'd held her weight against that archway as though she weighed nothing, attacked before she could assemble her defenses. Her mouth dried.

"It shouldn't have happened. I'll be more careful in the park next time." Her skin heated with another dose of that thick oily feeling in her veins. It wasn't a lie, but she wasn't ready to explain what else had led to her throwing up all the fluids she'd drunk yesterday. Not until she had to.

Setting aside the now full syringe on the metal rolling cart to collect various samples, Dr. Yarrow went back to the victim's mouth to collect DNA with an oversize Q-tip. "Well, pregnancy is certainly hard no matter where your health starts. Just let me know if I need to adjust your duties or your hours."

That… She hadn't expected that.

"What?" Drennan shook her head, no longer seeing the woman's face but a blur of white lab coat and darkening at the edges of her vision. She was holding her breath. Forcing herself to breathe through the surprise, she focused on capping the Q-tip Dr. Yarrow had swabbed and adding it to the sample cart. She'd just taken a pregnancy test yesterday morning and gotten her own confirmation. Her boss couldn't have known before her. Right? "How did you…"

"You've been more tired lately." The medical examiner didn't miss a step in their routine, inspecting the inside of the victim's mouth for wounds, missing teeth, crowns that might identify her or disease. The light coming from his magnifying glasses turned the woman's skin a waxy white. "Eating a lot more, too. I noticed you've been favoring more fresh fruit and vegetables."

"You concluded that I'm pregnant from all that?" Was that even possible? A new workout routine could end with those results.

Dr. Yarrow notched his head up to put her in his direct line of sight. The brightness of the light on his glasses skewered her vision. "Well, I might work with the dead, but I'm still around the living plenty. And I remember when my wife was pregnant. You wouldn't believe her cravings. Who voluntarily eats cottage cheese with watermelon?"

She didn't know what to say to that. She hadn't planned on telling him for a few more weeks and only because she'd need to take some time off after the baby came. Their work here wasn't strenuous, but she'd wanted to give him plenty of time to hire and train a new assistant if that was what he needed.

"Did you photograph these bruises on the back of her neck?" The medical examiner tilted the victim's head to one side, exposing the purple and blue marbling at her nape.

Drennan took as much of a cleansing breath as she could in a too-small exam room with a decomposing body that'd been out of the freezer for nearing two hours. "Yes. I already uploaded the photos to your laptop."

"These look like a handprint. Like someone held her

down and squeezed." Dr. Yarrow straightened with all that grace she'd never been able to achieve, even as a little ballerina, and tore his gloves free. He scratched at his nose with one thumb, his attention locked on the body. "Considering how long she was in the water, I can't imagine we'll get clean fingerprints off her skin, but the size of the handprint is a start. You said you couldn't find her ID?"

"No, and there are no missing person reports at this time. I was going to expand to other departments in the state, maybe even into Mesquite and Arizona to see if any of them filed a report matching her description later today."

"Something might come up on the X-rays. It's possible she's had surgery in the past and has a pin or plate with a serial number we can use. This is the fourth homicide I've seen in as few months coming out of that park." The medical examiner's eyes narrowed on their victim, and he removed his magnifying glasses. "It'll take a few more hours to finish the autopsy and at least three weeks for the crime lab to return the toxicology on the samples we've collected. I don't want to wait that long. Go back to the scene. See if you can find anything that tells us who she is. Make sure you take enough water this time and the waterproof gear. It's in the corner."

Back to the scene? Up the near three miles of incline and into water that looked like an algae breakout? And possibly run into the man she'd admitted to wanting more from? Oh, hell. Dread settled in the pit of her stomach, and a rush of acid charged into her throat. She swallowed it back, but like the thick oily feeling in her blood, it clung. This was her job. Her only source of income unless she wanted to burn through her savings. There were no other options from this point. She'd given them all up when she'd resigned from her position in the ER. No one would hire her back after what'd happened.

Drennan peeled her gloves free and tossed them into the biohazards wastebasket. Her breath shook on a long exhale. "I can do that."

She could. She'd done it once before. This time, she would be more prepared.

It took about twenty minutes to reach Zion National Park's front entrance and even less to park and catch the shuttle to the Grotto, where the Emerald Pool Trail began. Her legs burned from overuse on ascent, especially given the weight of the waterproof gear. Was Harvey assigned to patrol this trail today?

Her breath sawed in and out of her lungs with a burning at the back of her throat as she attacked the steplike boulders leading into the upper pools. Wasn't it rare for this area to be so empty of hikers? She'd bypassed a few on the ascent, but they'd been coming down from the pools. She'd expected a few hikers on the shore angling cameras up toward the hundred-foot waterfall blowing every which way from gusts as she donned the waterproof one-piece and boots. But this was good, too. There wasn't anyone to get in her way as she dredged the few-foot-deep pool.

"Ugh." Yeah. She was going to have to get in that water. For hours. Not how she intended her day to go. Drennan took her first step, surprised by the silt that gave way under her weight. She extended both arms for balance, then carefully tipped forward to get a better look into the murky water. Maybe she should've given Harvey or the other rangers a heads-up she'd come out to search the scene. They could've at least ensured she wasn't attacked by a pond monster, but the idea of seeing Harvey so soon after their last conversation... She needed time.

Piercing the surface with her net, she dragged the apparatus along the bottom of the pool. Coming up empty. There had to be something here. A phone, a wallet, the victim's ID very clearly identifying her remains. "Come on."

A shadow crossed the surface of the water to her left.

Drennan turned to warn the hiker not to get closer.

Lightning exploded across her vision. Along with the pain.

And then she was lost to the Emerald Pools.

Chapter Twelve

He hadn't been this nervous since reporting for basic training.

Harvey memorized the property through the windshield of his SUV. The Office of the Medical Examiner wasn't in a hospital or attached to the police station as other towns might've set it up. Nope. This one was in a freaking funeral home.

The bright white exterior was almost enough to convince him there weren't horrors waiting inside. Greek-like columns upheld the second story over an open walkway lining the entire structure with rows and beds full of pastel flowers and thick green shrubs. The property as a whole had obviously been well taken care of and designed to create a sense of peace in the visitors who walked through those elaborate double doors at the front.

Having the ME's office inside a funeral parlor made sense in a town with less than twenty-five thousand residents. Sort of. Both the ME and the funeral director handled remains. They both needed access to exam rooms, used refrigerators to stop decomposition and had all the tools that came with preparing a body for burial, but he couldn't shake the prickling dread at the back of his neck at the thought of walking in there. Not even for any big reason but a thousand little ones.

Most recently having to visit another funeral home on behalf of a man he honestly should've left to the state to bury.

But he wasn't here for that. He was here for Drennan. To apologize. To give her the respect she deserved. Because she was right. What he'd done—kissing her to convince her to give him what he wanted—was inexcusable, and he wasn't that man. Truly. Every cell in his body hated the idea she felt as though he'd turned her into a challenge to be conquered instead of the beautiful, caring, compelling woman she was. And she'd called him out on it, refused to get caught in self-imposed rules or used as a tool in some greater design. And, damn if that wasn't one of the sexiest things he'd ever seen, her putting him in his place.

I was just hoping for you.

He hadn't been able to stop repeating that single statement since the moment the words had left her mouth. Drennan didn't want his financial support. She'd wanted something more. And while he admired her ability to speak her mind and ask for what she wanted, it wasn't possible. He couldn't give her that. Not ever. She knew that, and yet… He couldn't stop thinking about the potential, either.

She wasn't just having *a* baby.

She was having *his* baby.

Maybe a boy who looked just like him with dark hair and wild blue eyes and got into all kinds of trouble wearing his mama down. Or a girl whose knowing green gaze that resembled a spring morning widened every time he walked through the door at the end of his day walking the trails. Laughter would fill his bare house as he scooped up his kid and spun them around until they were both dizzy.

Drennan would be there with that wide smile she seemed to reserve just for him, and he'd finally feel that tension in his chest release from being away from them when he dragged her mouth to his in greeting.

He could see it. Right there in front of him. All he had to do was reach out and grab that reality. Make it his. Drennan wanted that. Had admitted to wanting them to try.

But the image bled away to sharp reds and swallowing blacks, leaving nothing but the fitful nightmares of his childhood behind. To the bruises his mother had always caked in makeup to try to hide, to the scrapes and scabs on the backs of his dad's hands and the sickening smile on the old man's face when Harvey went out of his way to avoid getting anywhere near him. He could still feel the tightness in his arms and legs every once in a while, the automatic bracing at loud noises, to the point he thought his tendons might snap. A lot of those same bruises had found a way to him, his mother's begging and pleas going unheard as his father punished Harvey for some imagined slight. Low grades, not coming home from school fast enough, walking in front of the TV, not cleaning up his plate at the end of a meal. And while Harvey had found little ways to rebel against his dad, years of survival and pain had ingrained itself in his cells. It was part of him.

But he wouldn't let it touch her.

His fingers curled around the steering wheel, knuckles working to escape the backs of his hands. Harvey killed the ignition and forced himself from the SUV and through those doors. The too-sweet and stale floral scent filled the lobby in a cloying, invisible mist he'd have to work at to get rid of. Just like the last time he set foot in a funeral home, gleaming wood coffins angled and glinted across the sales floor, ranging in an array of colors and prices right down to a plain pine box. He'd chosen the cheapest option for his father because that was what the bastard deserved. Actually, he'd deserved less. Unfortunately, due to zoning laws burying the son of a bitch under the animal shelter to spend the rest of eternity getting crapped on wasn't possible. Though deserved.

But it wasn't until now Harvey realized he didn't know what his mother had been buried in, what his father had chosen to lay his wife of twenty-two years to rest in. Had there been a service? Flowers? Had anyone showed with their favorite casseroles to pay their respects to the woman who'd sacrificed her body and mental health to protect her son? He hadn't gotten more than a text message from his father letting him know she'd died and already been laid to rest. Taking that last ounce of hope she'd save herself.

His throat dried. A sign for the Office of the Medical Examiner at the front directed him to a set of stairs off to his right, leading down into the basement. The temperature dropped a few degrees with every step until he faced a set of wide steel doors. Shoving through, he pulled up short as a pair of terrifying oversize bug eyes locked on him. "What the hell?"

His skin tightened down his arms as he realized the magnifying glasses were worn by a light-haired man with a scalpel in one hand and a pair of tweezers in another. Other details started registering, too. Like the blood staining the front of the man's once white lab coat. And the female body stretched open on the table in front of him.

"Well, you're not supposed to be down here, Ranger Knight." Dr. Yarrow set aside his tools on a small rolling cart and peeled off his gloves before going for the lit magnifying glasses on his head. They'd met in the clinic parking lot to pass off the woman Harvey had recovered from the trail yesterday morning, but seeing the medical examiner in this light came with a whole new set of nightmare material he didn't need. "I assume you're here about our drowning victim?"

He wouldn't look at the remains on the table. He wouldn't look—

He looked. And, hell, he wished he hadn't. Wished he hadn't seen the victim's chest splayed open and pinned back like one of those butterflies he'd once seen spread out and framed in his boss's office. Harvey cleared his throat, feeling the blood drain from his face. "Sorry. I'm looking for Drennan. She working today?"

Dr. Yarrow came around the table, maneuvering in front of what Harvey could see of the victim and her insides. "She's out on an errand. If you're here about the autopsy of the victim recovered from the park, I won't have a final report for another few days. I still have multiple samples to be taken and organs to be weighed. Based on the bruises at the back of the victim's neck, I believe the manner of death is homicide by drowning. She was held under the water for several minutes, but we don't have an identity. That's why I sent Drennan back to the trail about an hour ago. We should have something for you soon."

"To the trail?" Warning signals exploded through him, and Harvey took one step farther into the exam room that smelled of fruity decay. Well, he certainly wished for the cloyingly thick scent of flowers now. "You sent her alone?"

"Ms. Hawes is more than capable of dredging the pond for the victim's personal effects on her own as well as determining if there is any evidence we need to consider for this investigation." The medical examiner grabbed for a new set of gloves. "Besides, I expect nothing less from a former trauma physician to be able to pick up the slack so

I can make it home for dinner on time for once. My wife tends to get sensitive if I am not where I am expected to be when I am expected to be."

Dr. Yarrow's smile crested and fell in equal time as he donned the new set of latex. "Is there anything else, Ranger Knight?"

"Have you heard from her?" He couldn't explain this simmering in his chest.

The medical examiner checked his watch, the lines between his brows deepening. "She should've checked in by now."

Harvey backed toward the door, a deep, resonating urgency taking hold in his blood. He had no doubt Drennan was far more qualified to collect any evidence at the scene than the rangers on staff, but knowing she was in the park alone—where a killer had recently murdered a lone hiker—didn't sit well. Of course, there was no evidence the killer would target an assistant medical examiner, but he couldn't get the warning bells in his head to quiet down. "Thanks."

He shoved through the double steel swinging doors meant to keep temperatures balanced on both sides and hauled himself up the stairs, rushing by the time he got to the top. He had no reason to think Drennan might be in danger, but some instinctual drive inside of him had Harvey jogging out of the building and to his truck and tearing out of the funeral home's parking lot. He'd given her his number to call in case of emergency with the pregnancy, but he hadn't saved hers. Navigating back to the highway, he headed straight for Zion, calling the visitor's center on the way.

The ranger on the other end hadn't seen or heard from the medical examiner's office, but the upper pool was still closed at Ranger Simpson's direction due to the investigation. Drennan must've bypassed the visitor's center and set out on the trail herself. Damn it. He should've reached out to her before now, but he'd wanted to give her space after their argument last night.

No. That wasn't it. His gut churned as the truth surfaced. He'd assumed she wouldn't want to talk to him, and her rejection... He didn't want that.

He put in a call to the head of the law enforcement division next for no other reason than to assure himself someone knew she was on that trail alone. The call connected.

"Simpson." The ranger's no-BS greeting didn't faze him one bit.

"It's Knight. That medical examiner we met yesterday at Emerald Pools. She reach out to you?" Harvey pressed down on the accelerator, his blood heating and humming in his veins. "Her boss sent her back to the trail to dredge the pond a little more than an hour ago. He hasn't heard from her since."

"Cell coverage is spotty up there, but no. I haven't seen her. I've got a ranger in the area. Give me a second. I'll have her check in." The silence on the other side of the line ratcheted Harvey's heart rate into dangerous territory. Two minutes. Three. Five? He lost sense of time, desert and sharp mountains ripping by as he navigated around slower vehicles down the highway toward Springdale.

"Knight, you're not going to like this." Simpson interrupted the chaos working to unravel him from the inside.

Harvey's entire body braced from a threat he couldn't even see coming, as automatic and painful as those nights his dad's footsteps were just a little bit louder than normal outside his bedroom door. He swallowed through it. "What happened?"

"Her gear is all there, man." The law enforcement ranger swore low enough Harvey didn't catch it. "But your medical examiner is not."

Chapter Thirteen

Her waterproof gear was no longer...waterproof.

And heavy. Or maybe gravity had doubled in the time since she'd died. Ugh. Drennan blinked against the on-slaught of sunlight overhead. Sheer cliffs rose up on either side of her, trees peppering her vision every few feet. Water spit into her face with a strong gust of wind. Her skin prickled with the sudden change in temperature. Twisting her head to one side, she cringed against the tender spot at the back of her head. The one pulsing with every beat of her heart. Water had infiltrated her gear. Her clothing clung to her frame, holding her down, hair plastered to her face and neck.

Fluffy white clouds skimmed across the sky overhead.

This wasn't the Emerald Pools trail.

Where the hell was she?

Wind kicked up a second time, spitting another few drops into her face. The short waterfall was nothing like the one that'd towered over her at the upper emerald pool. Drennan tried shoving to stand, though she didn't trust herself to make it far. Head injuries weren't like those in the mindless action movies and TV shows she liked to binge. There was no getting straight back up and walking off this trail like nothing had happened. Headaches, sensory issues such as vision and hearing, unconsciousness. Comas. She'd seen enough of them in the ER. Car accidents, assaults, domestic disputes.

Wait. Was that why she couldn't remember how she got here? No. She remembered…something. Pain speared through her head the harder she tried to recall the seconds leading up to waking here, but there was nothing more than a shadow. Had she passed out again? She sucked in a sharp breath. Was the baby okay?

Her wrists burned, the tendons in her shoulders pulling taut. She wrestled with whatever had pinned her hands. Then stilled. Drennan understood then. Why she couldn't push herself to sit up. Why her arms hurt and she couldn't remember how she'd gotten here.

Someone had hit her.

Someone had attacked her.

She'd gone to Emerald Pools to dredge the bottom of the pond for the victim's personal items, and… The shadow. It'd come up from behind. She hadn't gotten a chance to turn around before her attacker knocked her unconscious. Drennan struggled against the rope digging into her skin. It was dry compared to the rest of her. There wasn't any swelling to the strands, but it wouldn't budge. She wasn't strong enough to—

"I wouldn't do that if I were you." The voice sounded close and yet too far away at the same time. Like it'd set out to play a trick on her. Disembodied. No owner in sight. "You'll tear your wrists up real good that way."

Her breath guttered in her chest then pressurized until she was forced to release it. Scanning her surroundings, she studied every tree, every rock, every shift to pinpoint the source of the voice. "Who—"

"That's not the question you should be asking, Dr.

Hawes." The crunch of dirt and rock registered from be-hind. Footsteps.

The hair on the back of her neck stood on end. Unfil-tered warning exploded through her. Drennan twisted—too fast—aggravating the thudding pain in her head. The moan escaped without her permission, and she closed her eyes against the sudden brightness that lit up the back of her brain. One breath. Two. The pain receded slowly but surely. She forced her eyes open to keep her attacker in her line of sight, but it was too soon. Searing agony rip-pled across her head, and she had to close her eyes again, tripping the panic she could barely keep under control. She didn't like this. Being in a position of helplessness, of not knowing where the threat was coming from. Or from whom. There'd been too many times when her mother had doted on her, gone out of her way to include her and said all the things a mother should say to her daughter. It was disarming and promising. Only to have that hope ripped right out from under her.

His laugh worked to soothe the rough edges of her building anxiety against her will. Low and rolling, light considering the circumstances. She wasn't supposed to like it, but it reminded her of Harvey's. Deep and warm when he let go of thinking he was a monster.

"That had to hurt." That unexplainable sixth sense every human on the planet owned told her he'd taken up position in front of her. The small drop in temperature, too. He'd blocked the sun from beating down on her. "I was hoping to avoid this, but you have something that belongs to me. I would've gotten out of this hellhole free and clear if that ranger hadn't interrupted me."

Relief spread quick and fast as she attempted another glance at the man who'd hauled her off the Emerald Pools trail. He was tall. Taller than most of the men she'd known in her life, including her father and Dr. Yarrow. Thick beard growth and eyebrows matching dark hair—at least what she could see of it with the sun haloed around his frame—masked a large part his facial features. It didn't add to his attractiveness. It just made him look more weathered. Worn. He filled out his T-shirt well enough, though not nearly as well as most outdoorsmen. Pressed slacks that were stained with what she assumed were water spots and red dust from the trail had kept their crease as he crouched in front of her. Who in their right mind wore slacks out here? Well, other than park rangers. The sun was back in her eyes, and Drennan was forced to turn away, but she'd seen enough of his face she could identify him to police and the law enforcement rangers. If she got out of this in one piece.

Then his words registered. Her stomach flipped. Harvey. He was talking about Harvey. About discovering the body face down in the upper pool yesterday morning. Which meant… "You killed her. That woman who drowned."

"I warned her what would happen if she kept pushing." The weariness in what she now noted in his gray eyes aged him at least a decade right in front of her. "I didn't want to kill her, but she just wouldn't listen to reason. I had no other choice."

It took everything Drennan had left not to flinch against the familiar victimization of the predator in front of her. And even then, she failed. How many times had her mother played that part so well? Blamed Drennan for something that hadn't been her fault in the first place? Her mom's moods, her bad days, her grief, her life. How many times had Drennan internalized it? Tried to make things better?

Apologized for things she never should've apologized for just to avoid losing another piece of herself?

The man in front of her might have a different face, but Drennan identified the abuser beneath the mask. Knew that no matter what she said, he would never see himself as anything other than a reasonable man. Because in his head, he'd done no wrong. Her attacker caught the reaction, a slow smile spreading underneath all that beard growth a split second before he reached out for her.

She leaned back but was only able to go so far. His fingertips grazed her cheek, all the way down to her jaw, cold and alien. Her insides revolted at the touch. He was making her uncomfortable on purpose, trying to get a rise out of her when she'd spent so many years shutting down her emotions so they wouldn't be preyed upon. The rope seemed to tighten around her wrists, cutting off the blood flow to her fingers and digging into her low back.

"You remind me of her, you know." Wayward hair fell into his eyes as the wind kicked up, but he didn't bother to remove it. Almost like he didn't even realize it impaired his vision in the first place. So focused on her with a look she couldn't place. "She fought me, too. About everything. Where we would eat, which movie to watch, our future. It was one of the things I like about her the most."

A hint of grief charged into those steel gray eyes that seemed to contain several hundred years of thunderstorms, but it only lasted a minute.

"I don't…" She shook her head. "I don't know you. I don't have anything of yours."

"Sure you do." He shoved to stand, towering over her all over again. Every muscle in her body tightened at the prospect of all that power—that strength—turning against her. "You have her body."

Her… What? Air crushed from her chest.

"And if I can't get it from you, I'll get it from your colleague. Dr. Yarrow, right? I'm sure he wouldn't put up much of a fight." Her attacker slid his hands into his slacks pockets as though he'd done it a thousand times before, looking more comfortable in a boardroom or behind a desk rather than the middle of a national park, and it showed. The styling product in his hair had given up its fight, sweat darkening the collar of his shirt. An undershirt, she realized then. It didn't really go with pressed slacks, which meant he'd probably taken another shirt off somewhere. "Or that ranger you seem to like so much. Now, he seems like the kind of man who'd fight back, so I have no doubt whatever happened would get messy, but I've never shied away from getting my hands dirty, as you well know."

The blood drained from her face and neck. No. Acid surged up her throat. Not Dr. Yarrow. Not Harvey. While she'd learned to distance herself from others out of a sense of survival, she wasn't as heartless as former colleagues and friends had accused her of being. Dr. Yarrow had given her an opportunity to start over. He'd been nothing but supportive in the adjustment it'd taken for her moving to a new town and into a new position. He recognized her pregnancy symptoms and offered to be flexible in her work hours with understanding and compassion. She wouldn't let him get dragged into this. He had a family. A wife and grown kids that came around for Sunday dinners every week. A grandkid on the way.

And Harvey…

Her skin heated with blistering intensity. Harvey had gifted her something she'd never be able to repay. For one night, he'd chosen her. Made her feel wanted and beautiful. He'd looked at her as someone worthy and loved, not even having known her name at the time. Because that was the kind of man he was. Yes, he was brooding and unforgiving, but he'd been there when she'd needed him the most. Despite his internal hatred for the blood he carried in his veins and his fears of unleashing it on her and this baby, he'd been there without question. Took care of her as though she was the most important person in his life. He was brave. Braver than most. His father wouldn't have made that choice, and no one had done that for her since... Since her dad died. No one had willingly chosen her. But Harvey had, whether he accepted that fact or not. Just for a little while.

It was enough. For her to risk fighting back. For her to protect them from the predator closing in. He wouldn't get to them. Not ever. Whatever his plan, it wouldn't work.

Another dose of pain nearly dragged her under. The headache was getting worse, urging her to give in. Had she sustained a concussion? "Who are you?"

"A desperate man, Dr. Hawes." Her attacker wrapped a hand around her upper arm and hauled Drennan to her feet. Unforgiving muscle flexed under her palm as she worked to add distance between them, but it was no use. He was strong. Stronger than her. And he knew it. "Desperate men will do whatever it takes to get what they want. Remember that before you try to escape from me."

"But I thought you liked it when women fight back." Drennan put everything she had into the strike. Shoving her knee so far between his legs, she could've sworn she heard something burst. The impact threw her off balance, but she wouldn't let it stop her.

She ran.

Chapter Fourteen

His blood had reached a boiling point.

Harvey hauled himself up the last few step-like rocks leading up in the natural bowl carved out from the surrounding cliffs and up into the upper emerald pool. Ranger Simpson—Zion's head law enforcement division ranger— was already there with another Harvey didn't recognize. The rangers both faced him, their expressions hard as stone. He couldn't remember closing the distance between them. All he could focus on was the sheer panic eclipsing everything else in his body. He'd spent years under duress at home and in the military, and yet every single wall he'd built to keep himself in check crumbled in an instant. Harvey fisted both hands into Simpson's uniform, knocking the six-foot giant back. "Where is she?"

The words were more animalistic growl than human. The demon he'd been working on exorcising for as long as he could remember licked beneath the surface of his skin. He was too hot, too raw. Out of control.

The second ranger—he didn't get a look at her name tag—blew a bright pink bubble from the safety of a couple feet away. It popped, triggering his nerves to flinch. Her bleached blond hair threatened to get tangled in the gum she openly chewed. Other details bled into focus. A hot-pink kerchief around her throat, a matching manicure and the fact she'd switched out her standard issue laces for bright fuchsia. "You might not want to do that. Murray is capable of ripping each one of your fingers off and sticking them up your nose."

What? Harvey barely had the sense to think past the red haze turning him feral.

Strong hands gripped his wrists and clamped down. Steely eyes pinned Harvey in place, but the threat of danger was nothing compared to the tumult swirling in his gut. "I know what you're feeling right now, Ranger Knight. I've lived through that crushing feeling of guilt and concern, to the point you have trouble taking your next breath, but if you don't remove your hands, I will do exactly what Ranger Jordan has suggested. Or something as equally creative. She's very good at coming up with death threats, and I've always wanted to test one."

"It's true. I'm trying to come up with the perfect one for him to try. Right now, we're thinking about touching someone's face with a shovel. Really hard." Too-white teeth flashed across the woman's face, and Harvey realized this was the one other rangers had called Ranger Barbie for so long. He hadn't worked with her directly before she'd joined the law enforcement rangers, and he sure as hell wasn't interested in working with this too bright, chaotic rainbow of a woman. "You want to try one? It might help with all that—" she motioned to his face "—tension."

"I don't care." It took everything in Harvey to release his hold. Violence had been ingrained in his blood, in every muscle he owned from a young age. Beaten into him since his first memory. It was how things got done, and he'd so easily slipped back into that place he wanted to forget. Into the man he didn't want to be. But he would.

He'd give up everything for Drennan and the baby, to give them a chance to be free of him. Oxygen seemed to thin with every controlled inhale, but it wasn't enough. "Where is Dr. Hawes?"

"Not here." Ranger Simpson smoothed down the collar of his shirt, erasing the lines Harvey had pressed into it with his grip. "We've got her gear left unattended. We found a duffel bag and a net in the pool, but no medical examiner. Ranger Jordan just returned from searching the lower pools as well as the trail that continues up and around the waterfall."

"And?" His entire body hung on an answer he wasn't sure he wanted.

"No sign of her." Ranger Jordan had lost that too bright quality with the change in subject, becoming the law enforcement ranger this park—that he—needed, though her high pigtails sat in opposition to every word out of her mouth. "But I made out a set of footprints. Large. Most likely male. One set heading toward the pool, a deeper, identical set going back the way they came from through those trees."

She nodded to the expanse of wilderness behind him. There was no official trail there. Nothing but miles and miles of open terrain. "We believe the treads are deeper due to the fact he was carrying something heavier than when he entered this area."

"Drennan." Harvey closed his eyes against the very real possibility of losing something he'd never even had. Something he'd fought against from the very beginning. "Who the hell would want to take an assistant medical examiner?"

Ranger Simpson shook his head, crossing his arms over a too large chest more than capable of following through on whatever death threat Ranger Jordan came up with. "The trail has been closed off since you discovered the body yesterday. Whoever it was didn't stick to the public access. They had to have come from backcountry, which means—"

"They were waiting for her." Harvey set sights on the gear Drennan had left behind. The duffel bag, the net. Dr. Yarrow had sent her to collect any evidence that might supply them with the victim's name. "Or someone from the medical examiner's office."

"I have rangers gearing up to search the wilderness, but it'll take time." Simpson shifted on his feet, obviously as eager to get out there as fast as possible, but there were procedures. Protocols and clearances they had to follow. Not to mention, they had no idea what kind of threat they might be facing out there. "Time your ME might not have."

The law enforcement ranger was right. Every second Drennan was out there—alone, potentially injured or worse—was another opportunity her abductor had to ensure Harvey never saw her again. And that…wouldn't happen.

"She's not mine." He'd told Drennan the same thing, hadn't he? That nothing could happen between them. It was too dangerous. A future full of nothing but misery and pain, and yet the thought of watching her move on with someone else… Because she would. She'd meet someone new, someone who didn't come with a whole bunch of red flags enough to stock a carnival. Who wanted to be with her and would have no problem raising another man's child. Because she was worth it. Because her smile—the genuine one she didn't show often—didn't just light up a whole damn room. It lit up pieces of himself Harvey was convinced had been brutalized out of him a long time ago.

Who in their right mind wouldn't fall for a woman like that? In the few short hours Drennan had spent with him, she'd believed him to be a better man than he was. Told him he wasn't his father without knowing a single thing about him. Trusted him to take care of her, to take care of their baby, to reveal parts of herself he doubted many knew about.

"Whatever you say, Knight." Simpson eyed him as though he'd backed a feral animal into a corner and was worried for the coming fight.

And, hell. Harvey was feeling more than a little feral at the moment, but he wouldn't let it get to him. Not while she was out here alone. How? How was it possible she'd become central and indispensable in his life in such a short amount of time? He wasn't a backcountry ranger, but his military training supplied enough experience to prepare him for anything. Including the worst-case scenario. "I need a survival pack. Any one of yours will do."

He caught the trepidation in Ranger Simpson's expression. Right before the ranger motioned for his companion to give them some space. "As the head of the law enforcement division, I'm supposed to say it would be better if you waited for the search team."

"I'm not waiting." He didn't give a damn about rank or orders or anything else that might keep him from bringing Drennan and the baby back safely.

"You didn't let me finish." Simpson stepped in close, lowering his voice. "I said I'm *supposed* to say it would be better for you to wait for Search and Rescue and follow protocol. Except I know that look and the thoughts racing through your head. Knowing she's out there, that she needs you, is going to drive you into near madness. Use it. You're the best chance she has of surviving whatever that bastard has planned for her."

Harvey didn't know what to say to that. What to think. The division head of the law enforcement rangers was voluntarily overriding protocols put into place to keep rangers and hikers alike alive. Why? "You sound like you're speaking from experience."

Ranger Simpson glanced over Harvey's head, as though expecting a whole new threat to come crashing through the trees on the other side of the trail. The unfocused blur in his gaze disappeared so fast Harvey wasn't sure if he'd imagined it. "I am."

Ranger Jordan returned, two black backpacks in hand. She tossed one to him, which he caught against his chest, keeping the second pack for herself. "Try to keep up. We've got a lot of ground to cover and not a lot of time to do it in." She cut her attention to her supervisor. "You ready for the hell that's coming your way?"

"I'll cover for you." Simpson uncrossed his arms, facing off with Ranger Jordan, not in the least bit intimidating despite his size. Well, at least not toward the woman less than half his size. "Branch won't know you're going off the reservation, but don't make me explain how you ended up dead. None of us will survive that. Check in every hour with your location. I'll hold him off as long as possible. Channel four."

She gave an exaggerated salute and headed for the trees. "Good luck."

Harvey extended one hand in a peace offering meant to make up for the aggression still rolling through him. "Thank you."

"It's nothing." Simpson took his hand. "I wouldn't wish that madness on my worst enemy, but I wasn't lying when

I said it will give you the best chance of recovering Dr. Hawes. She's obviously important to you. Use it."

Harvey didn't feel like explaining to the law enforcement ranger he'd spent the better part of his life doing just that. Using the poison in his blood to survive, to fight back and to carry out his orders had made it easier to call on it each time. Until he wasn't sure he'd ever be rid of that demon he hated so much. And with Drennan... Damn it, Simpson was right. She'd become important, but Harvey never wanted her or the baby to see that part of him. Ever.

He followed in Ranger Jordan's footsteps, nearly in a jog as they met up with the treads she'd identified earlier. Tree branches scratched at his face, neck and forearms as they ran deeper into the backcountry. No landscaped trails. No packed dirt to make the hike easier. Out here, every tree, rock and stream could kill them without warning. The sky remained a crystal clear blue and didn't promise heavy rains that would wash the evidence of Drennan's abduction out. They'd be able to use the tracks to hunt down the man who'd taken Drennan as far as they could. Maybe straight to her.

His blood hummed as they picked up the trail. He clung to the pack's straps to keep it from bouncing, increasing his speed despite nature's determination to slow him down. Drennan had been taken, but he'd get her back. Her and the baby. There was no other option.

His father had taken away everything. Choice, freedom, his sense of worthiness, hope. But the son of a bitch couldn't take the one bright light in his life or the memories that came with it. He couldn't take Drennan.

All Harvey had to do—when, not if, they brought her back—was reach out and claim her for himself. Claim their future. If he was brave enough to take the risk.

Chapter Fifteen

Fatigue was a real bitch.

Every muscle she'd forgotten she owned—all of which she'd memorized during years of medical school—screamed in protest with each step forward. Drennan had lost sight of any hint of a trail an hour ago, heading through miles and miles of tall trees, jagged rocks and the biggest mountains she'd ever seen. More than an hour? Time had no meaning out here in the middle of nowhere. She wasn't sure which direction she'd run, how far or how long. At the time, all she'd been thinking about was escape.

Well, she'd done a hell of a job at that.

She was so turned around, not even a killer could find her out here.

But she didn't dare stop. No matter how hard her stomach twisted with hunger, how blistered her feet or burned her scalp and face. How could she have been so blind? She was lost. In the middle of a national park with no food, no water, no supplies of any kind. She'd never been allowed to join the Girl Scouts or go camping with the other girls in her local church. She didn't know the first thing about wilderness survival, except apparently what not to do.

Sweat had stopped beading at her hairline and the back of her neck and had now gotten trapped in her clothing and gear. Fall brought lower temperatures in most areas of the country. In Ohio this time of year, it'd be on the low end of forties, but Zion itself was so far south, it felt like she'd descended straight into hell.

Tendrils of scrub brush scraped against her waterproof bodysuit, slowing her down. Her gear was weighing her down, draining her of the last remnants of energy. And, thanks to the baby, she didn't have that much to begin with. Not like she'd had any real choice. Running had been the only option. Otherwise, her body might've been the next Harvey found on the trail.

Drennan forced herself to take the next step. And the one after that. But her shoe slipped off the smooth surface of the rock underfoot and jutted to one side. Her whole ankle angled outward, taking her body weight, and she went down. The ground rushed up to meet her, and she threw her bound hands out, doing what she could to avoid face-planting. The impact jarred through her right side. Gravel and dirt embedded in her palms, and pain light-ninged into her right hip. She'd managed to absorb most of the fall onto one side instead of her middle, but the agony refused to relent. Insects quieted at the sound of her gasp, throwing her into bone-chilling silence.

If the killer had been following her, he'd most likely heard it.

Peeling herself from the ground, Drennan spit the dirt that'd forced its way into her mouth. Her weight shifted enough to reignite the pain in her side. One of the jagged rocks she'd been trying to avoid had cut through her water-proof suit. No signs of blood. That was good. The chances of infection out here—without a first aid kit—were higher than she wanted to think about, but the injury would slow her down nonetheless.

Hell. She didn't even know where she was going. Which direction she'd started running. She remembered one of the psychologists back in Ohio checking a patient for cognitive issues who'd taken a tumble down Mount Airy—the only real mountain hiking around Cincinnati—telling nurses about the brain's tendency to walk in circles in open spaces. Even with use of all five senses and determination to walk a straight line, humans had a tendency to veer right or left, bringing them in circles. Was that what was happening now? Drennan didn't think so, but it was impossible to tell which rocks she'd already passed, if that was the same tree she'd passed before or if she was putting herself back in range of a man determined to use her to get to his first victim.

She wished Harvey was here.

Dryness coated the back of her throat. The sinking sensation that came with that thought pulsed in time with the beat in her right hip. He'd know what to do. He'd have supplies to help. Because it was literally his job. He'd keep her focused, help her get back to civilization. He'd make her feel safe, as he had that night in the bar. She hadn't told him, but she'd known he would've stepped in if she'd needed help warning off the guy who'd approached her. That was just the kind of man he was. Aware of others. Ready to take action if needed. He was a good man, even if he didn't believe it himself. She didn't know any abusers who would've taken her home to give her time to recover from passing out, and the ones she did would've ensured that a small price was paid later down the line, hanging that favor over her head for eternity. But that wasn't Harvey. He hadn't asked for anything from her in return or gone out of his way to remind her of what he'd done for her benefit, and she…wasn't used to that. Being taken care of by someone else was new, but she liked it. She liked him.

Testing her weight on her ankle, Drennan nearly buckled a second time, catching herself against a tree. Rough bark cut into her palms along with the gravel and dirt already doing their job.

She'd screwed this up so bad. Dr. Yarrow had sent her on a simple assignment. Collect any personal items or evidence their victim might've left behind at the scene to help identify the remains. Instead, she'd gotten herself abducted and now couldn't hike her way out of a wet paper bag. If she didn't come across a ranger or another hiker—something, anything—soon, she would die out here. There was no question. She pressed one hand over the cut in her suit, aggravating the sensitive tissue underneath. Most likely a bone bruise. Not lethal but intense enough to steal her breath. She would live. For a little while longer, anyway.

"It's okay. It's going to be okay. We're going to get out of here." Her hand automatically smoothed across her midsection. Directly above that little bundle of cells with the power to change her life. Had changed her life. Whether that change was for worse or better, she didn't know yet. But she wanted to find out. She wanted the opportunity, to have something that was just hers. A chance to love something unconditionally without the threat of it being taken away or used against her. She wanted a family again.

So she had to stop, to think about this. Continuing on through Zion's backcountry without any supplies or food would only kill her faster. Adrenaline had long worn off. She hadn't registered any hints of the killer for the past hour, though she was sure it wasn't hard for even a novice hunter to follow her tracks at this point. Maybe he'd given up. Decided she wasn't worth it. But that only meant he'd turn his deadly intentions onto Dr. Yarrow. Or Harvey.

Drennan sank back against the tree. Sharp edges dug into her spine as she slid onto her rear. The sun angled into the canyon, built by two impossibly tall walls of sheer red rock, from her left. Okay. That meant the sun was arching into the west, right? So it was past noon, and she was facing…north. Though there wasn't much to see from her current position. She'd been running east with the sun at her back, she didn't know how long, but it had to have been three hours—maybe four—at least. She'd parked at the visitor's center around ten in the morning and gotten to the upper emerald pool around eleven. She tried recalling the layout of the park from the few times she'd picked up a map and thought about getting out into nature as part of this whole new life thing she had going, but that'd been months ago. It was no use.

Someone had to realize she was missing, right?

Dread pooled at the base of her spine. Dr. Yarrow would clock out precisely at five and most likely assume she'd done the same after collecting whatever evidence she could find from the trail. Or presume she'd needed more recovery time from yesterday due to the pregnancy he was very much aware of. No one had been at the base of the trail or at the scene when she'd arrived. Only signs had designated the Emerald Pools trail closed to the public until the ME's office and the law enforcement rangers had what they needed for the investigation into the victim's death. And Harvey… She hadn't heard from him since she'd walked out his front door last night. She'd wanted to give him time to think about this whole them-having-a-baby-thing, but what she'd really done was run away from potential rejection like the coward her mother had always accused her of being.

Nobody knew she was out here.

Nobody would know she was missing.

And the voicemail her only remaining parent—a woman who was supposed to love her—had left on her phone the night she'd been driven to the bar replayed in her head. *You're going to die alone. Nobody will care that you're gone. You think you get to be happy by leaving me here all alone? Your father believed in fairy tales, too. Look what happened to him.*

Well, her mom was finally right about something, wasn't she?

She closed her eyes against the vile words stuck in her head, setting her head back against the tree bark. Her mother hadn't always been so bitter. She'd been happy once, in love. Whole. There'd been weekend road trips to the lakes and the movies, big birthday parties and Christmases, family dinners every night and help with homework when she needed it. Smiles and laughter, inside jokes and flirtatious teasing. Drennan had always feigned gagging when her parents had kissed, but deep down, she'd wanted that too someday. Her own family and all the joy that came with it.

But grief did terrible things to the heart and soul.

It corrupted all those happy memories into someone Drennan didn't recognize anymore. Someone who'd turned on her own daughter because the pain had become too much to handle alone.

A twig snapped nearby.

Drennan forced her eyes open despite her body being more than happy to give in to the tug of sleep, and a surge of awareness gave her new energy. Every sense she owned strained for the hint of something tangible to grab onto, but the trees were still. The insects had gone quiet again. Nothing moved. She wanted to trust her senses, but her brain was telling her to get up. To run.

Pressure built in her chest the longer she dared to hold her breath. Putting weight into her left leg, she bit against the flare of discomfort and slid herself back up the tree. The ache was deeper now, swelling through her entire hip, but she couldn't think about that right now.

The hairs on the back of her neck stood on end.

Drennan backed away from the tree she'd collapsed against, blindly navigating into the open. It might not be the smartest move, but she'd have a much better chance of running without having to maneuver through packed trees or going too far off course.

Keeping her gaze on the surrounding wilderness, she let the tension bleed out of her shoulders. There wasn't anyone there. Just a falling branch or—

"Hello, Dr. Hawes." Muscled arms pulled her against a wall of human granite. Her scream cut off with a slap of her attacker's hand over her mouth. "I've been looking for you."

Chapter Sixteen

They'd lost the tracks.

Harvey's legs threatened to give out from under him, the muscles along the backs screaming for relief, but he only pushed himself harder. Forced himself to take that next step and the one after it. It was all he could focus on to keep himself from spiraling down into raw desperation. Drennan was out here. She'd been abducted—his baby had been abducted—and he and Ranger Jordan were her only hope of bringing her back. The boot treads they'd followed ended at a stream crossing that branched off the upper emerald pool. Harvey had searched every inch of that riverbed, but the tracks had simply disappeared.

His blood thundered—too hot—in his veins. "They couldn't have just vanished."

"I've searched at least a hundred feet downstream and back on both sides. The treads don't reappear." Ranger Jordan hauled her pack higher up her back by the straps. "We're assuming these tracks belong to Drennan's kidnapper, and if that's the case, I think we're dealing with someone knowledgeable of wilderness survival and hunting."

Understanding hit as Harvey studied the stream. It wasn't any deeper than a few inches with smooth stones staring up through clear moving water. Unhurried and pristine this deep into the park. It wasn't until the stream reached the Emerald Pools that algae and a whole lot of other organisms latched on. But here, it was perfect with the whisper of the wind off the cliffs, the birds and insects trilling nearby and sun glinting off the surface of the water. He shook his head. "He moved into the stream to make sure we couldn't gauge which direction he'd gone."

"Chances are he hasn't double backed toward the pools, but that still leaves us with two separate directions to search along the stream." Ranger Jordan twisted her head to one side, as though looking for the right answer, and her hot pink kerchief dipped down her neck, revealing the thick, jagged scar beneath. "If our guy still has Dr. Hawes, he'll be moving more slowly, maybe even stop somewhere out of the way to camp depending on his ability to make her comply. Search and Rescue will have arrived on the scene by now. They'll have more manpower and search capacity than us running up and down this riverbed blind. We should wait."

Harvey wanted to ask about the scar, wanted to know who'd done something so horrific to her and if they'd suffered, but now wasn't the time. As much as he didn't know about Drennan and her outdoor experience, the pregnancy and this heat would take more out of her than she could spare to fight back. Her attacker would use the exhaustion against her and get the upper hand, and Harvey was betting she hadn't brought supplies other than those the law enforcement rangers had recovered at the upper pool. He checked his watch. They'd already been out here for close to an hour and a half with no additional signs of where she'd been taken.

She could be anywhere. In any kind of condition.

He swiped sweat from his brow, his clothes sticking to

him with layers of sweat and salt. Harvey shook his head. He'd had plenty of water. Anything he had left would be reserved for Drennan when he found her. "She doesn't have that kind of time. We can't search this entire river one direction at a time. We need to split up. You head east. I'll head west. Stick to the streambed, call in anything you find on the radio."

Every cell in his body honed in on that one purpose. To find Drennan. Now. It latched on to every thought and drove the lactic acid buildup in his muscles to a dull sting. He'd already failed her enough to haunt him for the rest of his life. He couldn't leave her out here to fight alone.

Ranger Jordan stepped in, dragging her water bottle from her pack and sucking down a strong mouthful before returning it to the compartment at the side of her bag. "Trail rangers aren't trained to confront a suspect. I am, and I'm armed. We don't know who's behind Dr. Hawes's abduction or if he's carrying a weapon. It's enough we have one missing person. We can't have you disappear on top of that."

"You're right. Trail rangers aren't trained to confront suspects, but soldiers are." That training was already taking hold. Sinking deep into his nervous system. Calming his heart rate and spreading a numbness he hadn't let himself feel in a long time. It was the same kind of numbness his father sank into right before the son of a bitch exploded. The calm before the storm, but Harvey was willing to do whatever—to become whatever—he needed to find Drennan. To bring her back alive. "Don't worry about me. If splitting up comes back on you, tell Simpson it was my idea, and you tried to stop me."

He turned west, keeping to the riverbed as Drennan's abductor would. No longer looking to escape the predator hiding under his skin. He wanted it right at the surface. Whoever'd taken Drennan had a few tricks up his sleeves.

Water lapped around his boots, quiet and unchallenged, as he followed the stream. He didn't want to give away his presence too soon, not knowing how a scared animal would react to surprise. He couldn't risk the kidnapper deciding Drennan wasn't worth the effort and doing something rash. That familiar heat he'd run from most of his life built with every yard gained, his senses tapped out. The birds had quieted with his passing, as though sensing an apex predator had neared. Harvey didn't have any weapons. He didn't need them, but that didn't mean whoever had abducted Drennan had the same beliefs. And if she was hurt... He stopped the growl rumbling through his chest. He couldn't think about that right now.

He'd consciously made decisions in exact opposition to his father over and over. Anger management, self-help books, therapy, keeping his emotions under control in even the most dire situations, strict routines, isolating himself to protect others. The women he'd been with over the years had been nothing more than passing interests. Purely physical. They'd known there wouldn't be anything more once they parted ways. No dates or vacations. No meeting the parents or talk of the future. He'd done whatever he had to in order to keep himself from becoming the man he hated most, the man who'd ultimately killed Harvey's mother because he'd been too weak to control himself.

And it'd been enough. For a while.

Right up until two months ago when he'd seen her from across the bar and recognized the same haunted look in Drennan's eyes that stared back at him from the mirror every morning. And he'd wanted her. More than he'd wanted anyone or anything in his life. He'd wanted to make the shadows in her pretty green eyes fade, to know who or what had put them there and to make sure they never touched her again. And he had. For a little while at least. And she'd done the same for him. He'd looked in the mirror the next morning and almost hadn't recognized himself. The heaviness that'd aged him in a matter of days after learning about his father's death had lifted. His gaze had been brighter, some color had come back into his face, but more, something inside had shifted. Released to the point he felt as though he could breathe for the first time in years.

Drennan had done that. And he'd gone and thrown that gift back in her face when she'd told him she was pregnant. What would his father have done? Hell, his dad would've made sure that child—and the woman carrying it—suffered. That they both broke under the sick bastard's influence until they were just as miserable as Harvey and his mother.

But he wasn't his father. He didn't get his rocks off at a woman crying at his feet or a child stepping in front of its mother to protect her. He didn't enjoy putting others' lives at risk or seeing how little it took to manipulate people into fearing him. He didn't want any of that, and he sure as hell wouldn't ever lay his hands on an innocent woman or their child.

Harvey wasn't that man, and Drennan… She was everything he'd ever wanted. She was the dream he'd dared to envision all those times he'd let himself think of the future, of escape, of being anywhere but stuck under his father's thumb. She was strong and caring with a smile that could knock him off balance. A woman who enjoyed giving pleasure as much as she enjoyed experiencing it and went out of her way to stand up for herself and the peo-

ple she cared about. Drennan Hawes was intelligent beyond belief with a sharp tongue that could eviscerate him
in a single sentence while putting other people ahead of
herself. Dependable and kind and soothing in a way he'd
never experienced to the point she risked burning herself
out just to make sure everyone else had what they needed.

A woman like that needed someone who would step in
and put her first. A protector to make sure she didn't give
too much of herself, that she was getting enough to eat and
reminding her to go take a bath or a nap when things got
to be too heavy for her to carry alone. And, damn, Harvey found himself wanting to be that guy. He needed to
be that for her and for the baby to destroy the sins of his
father, but he had to find her first.

Pressure wedged between his shoulder blades. Slowing
to a stop right there in the middle of the stream, he listened
to his surroundings for a series of breaths. His fingers
twitched at his side. He hadn't held a gun in a long time,
but something about being watched from behind brought
back the need for the comfort warm steel provided. Nothing had changed. Birds still flew overhead. The stream
hadn't altered course apart from around his boots. He saw
nothing to get his defenses raised, but his instincts told him
he wasn't alone. Harvey craned his chin over one shoulder. There. Movement in the corner of his vision, behind
the copse of trees to his right. "You take her?"

"Gotta say, she didn't make it easy." That dark outline
keeping to the trees shifted. "But if I'm being honest, I'm
surprised you're here alone. Figured SAR would be all up
my ass on this one, but NPS has so much red tape to cut
through, it's a wonder anything gets done around here."

SAR. NPS. That was a whole lot of acronyms for a random man kidnapping a medical examiner. Tension bled

into Harvey's shoulders. Drennan had fought back, but how much had the son of a bitch made her pay for that choice? He didn't recognize the owner of the voice as he faced the threat head-on. "Where is she?"

"Safe. For now. And you. I know who you are, Ranger Knight." Dress slacks that'd lost their clean lines hung off the man's waist. He was tall, maybe taller than Harvey, but not as developed in other areas. His T-shirt was too tight and darkened with sweat around the collar and under his arms, and Harvey just didn't like the look of his face with all that gray beard growth and slicked-back hair. Like the guy couldn't stop running his hands through it. Drennan's abductor reached behind him, pulling a gun. Taking aim at Harvey as he descended the slight dip toward the stream. In a matter of feet, the gun barrel pressed into Harvey's chest. "Dr. Hawes is going to run a little errand for me. Until I'm done with her, I suggest you turn around and walk back the way you came."

Harvey scanned the trees, searching for something— anything—that could lead him to Drennan. "You know who I am? My background?"

The bastard nodded.

"Then you know you have exactly three seconds to put the gun down and bring me Drennan." Harvey had had plenty of weapons pointed at and used against him. He was prepared for whatever came next. "One. Two."

He didn't wait. Harvey slammed his palm over the barrel of the weapon and ripped the gun free of its owner. Turning it back around, he dropped the magazine and cleared the chamber, tossing the gun a few feet away. "Three."

"I think I'm going to like facing off with you, Ranger Knight." Hands raised, the abductor smiled as he backed up the incline and slightly to the left. The bastard was running. "But it seems today is not that day."

In seconds, the abductor had disappeared over the sharp incline leading into deeper backcountry, leaving Harvey alone.

"Drennan!" He hauled himself up the easy hill and into the trees, his chest tight and pressurized. "Dren—"

Soft curves overrun by navy-blue gear and long hair sticking to bark materialized at the base of a tree. Her arms had been secured behind her, her chin nearly to her chest with her legs splayed in front of her. Alive. She had to be alive.

His heart threatened to break his rib cage as he charged the tree and pulled a blade from his pack. Cutting through the rope binding her wrists around the tree, he caught her upper body from collapsing forward. "Drennan, open your eyes."

Unfocused eyes the color of the water in the Emerald Pools flickered open. Her gaze settled on him, and the invisible monster beneath his skin curled up and lay down for the first time…ever. Her voice broke. "You're not supposed to be here."

She slipped back into unconsciousness.

Chapter Seventeen

The curtain cutting her off from the rest of the ER snapped back.

"I'm getting tired of seeing you in a hospital bed." Cassidy brought her attention up from her clipboard and used her foot to drag the bedside stool behind her. There seemed to be a few more lines around her friend's eyes and mouth as she looked Drennan over, and a similar heaviness responded in Drennan's chest.

She'd been abducted. Could've died if it hadn't been for Harvey. Between learning of the pregnancy, coming to terms with Harvey's self-imposed banishment in hers and the baby's lives and getting knocked unconscious by the man who obviously had no qualms when it came to killing a woman, she could only shove the terror she'd felt—and still felt—down deep where it would never see the light of day again.

"You and me both." Her gear and clothing had been confiscated as evidence by Zion's law enforcement rangers. She'd been offered a set of scrubs by one of the nurses who'd learned she used to be an ER physician, and it'd taken much longer than it should have to change. Every major muscle in her body burned in protest of movement until she'd given up trying to do anything herself and finally asked the nurse to help get some pants on. The sea-foam green did nothing to hide the purple and blue blotches around her wrists and along one side of her face. Exhaustion had been trying to pull her under since Harvey had carried her out of the backcountry and down the trail as she'd clung to him like a koala bear, but she wouldn't give in. Not until she knew the baby was okay. "Tell me I don't look like a piece of bruised fruit."

"I'm not comfortable lying to patients." Cassidy took a seat on that rolling stool and got up close and personal with a penlight aimed directly at Drennan's face. "You know the drill."

Pain arched through her face and deep into her brain at the sudden brightness. Drennan followed the penlight as best she could.

Cassidy watched her pupils for the automatic response to light stimulant, but didn't give anything away in her expression. "Headache?"

"Yes." There was no way she could deny it at this point. Every change in sound or light had punctured her brain as thoroughly as an ice pick to the skull. It'd been a miracle the hit she'd taken to the back of the head hadn't killed her. Drennan didn't let herself touch the soft swell pulsing in time to her heartbeat. The stitches were fresh, and, if she was being honest, she wasn't up for another round of searing agony.

"Blurry vision?" Her friend clicked the light off—thank goodness—and made a quick note in the chart with the other end of her pen. Dry, cracked skin told of countless rounds of hand washing, disinfectant and latex gloves while Cassidy's sunken cheeks testified to long hours, late nights and very little sleep. Was that why their conversation felt so forced?

It took more energy than Drennan had to spare not to demand her friend look at her like a person and not just another patient. To see her. "Not at the moment."

"Hallucinations?" Cassidy ticked off another box on the head trauma questionnaire while everything inside of Drennan went cold.

Her exhale sounded overly loud in the small space, considering the ER was currently packed to the brim with patients, darting nurses and overworked techs. "Yes. I thought my friend walked in here, but it turns out she's been replaced by a pod person."

Cassidy raised a perfectly arched brow. Another second passed before the ice melted from her expression and a soft smile curled at one corner of her mouth. This was the woman who'd jumped to help at the first sign Drennan wasn't okay. The one who'd gone out of her way to recommend her for a job without question, to give her that push she needed to escape Ohio and finally take control of her life. "This is serious, Drennan. You were abducted. You…you could've died out there. I know you're used to having to take care of everyone else over yourself, but I need you to put yourself first for once. For the people who care about you."

Thickness coated the sides of Drennan's throat. She didn't want to acknowledge how much those words meant to her—that someone cared about her—because doing so meant acknowledging how much all the other words hurt. The ones that said her own mother had wished Drennan had been the one to die instead of her father in that accident, that having children had been a mistake or that she was responsible for all the misery in her mom's life. "Where is Harvey?"

"Your ranger was about to bring down the entire building pacing the ER, so I sent him to the cafeteria to get you something to eat for when you woke up. I have a feeling holding still isn't in his repertoire." Cassidy set the clipboard, the pen and the concussion questionnaire aside, that serious look back in her eyes. "You were unconscious for about three hours after he brought you in. The blunt force to the back of your head resulted in a concussion. Any harder, and you wouldn't be here."

She'd known that. How close she'd come, but her abductor had wanted her incapacitated to get what he wanted. Not dead. Though she wouldn't be thanking him anytime soon.

"He's not my ranger." Another burst of pain speared through her head. Dragging one hand across her forehead, she dug her thumb into her eye to relieve the pressure.

"Really? Because you were pretty out of it, but it took two of us to pry you off of him." Cassidy's smile widened. "I think you tore his shirt."

"Must've been the trauma." Because she sure as hell wouldn't cling to Harvey Knight for any other reason. He'd made his intentions with her and the baby clear, and she was nothing if not a champion for boundary setting. No matter how much she wanted things to be different between them, she couldn't live in another one-sided relationship. Getting out of the last one had nearly destroyed her. "I take it you've already done a CT scan to discount any brain bleeds, or I wouldn't be recovering in the ER." Her fingers ached as though she'd been clenching something for days rather than the past few minutes of keeping her hands busy with the seams of the sheets. "I'd like an ultrasound to check on the baby."

"Already ordered. The ob-gyn should be down in a few minutes to take a look." The stool gave a high-pitched squeak as Cassidy shoved back. "Do you remember if you suffered any trauma to your torso or belly?"

Drennan smoothed her hands down her front, resting them against her lower half as if she could add some semblance of protection. Which was ridiculous. She'd only just found out she was pregnant yesterday. She shouldn't have this level of…attachment yet, but the small bundle of cells had become her entire world overnight. She'd do anything to keep it. "Uh, no. I'm not sore or bruised that I can tell. I don't think he… I don't think things got that far."

But they could have. Her attempt to protect Dr. Yarrow and Harvey had nearly gotten her killed. It'd been reckless and a choice she would probably make a second time, but she couldn't just think about herself anymore.

A shiver danced across her shoulders as a man-shaped outline materialized at the foot of her bed. Carrying a tray of food. Her breath crushed from her chest at the sight of his wrinkled uniform shirt and slacks. Dark hair had escaped its normal styling, an equally frantic look in his gaze.

"Hi." Her voice barely carried through the small, private section the curtain provided in the bustling ER, but Harvey seemed to straighten at the sound. Images of the last time she'd talked with him flashed in rapid succession—her admission to wanting more between them, him revealing the truth about his father, declining his financial support for the baby. She'd left him standing in the middle of his living room, determined to do this on her own. But she would've died if it hadn't been for him. She knew that now. That her abductor had wanted her for a very specific reason and that when he was finished with her, she most likely would've ended up face down in a pool of water just like his last victim.

"Hey." That single word sounded as though it'd been pulled over hot coals. Lifting the tray of food, he cut his attention to Cassidy and back. "Figured you'd be hungry when you woke up."

"You mean your trip to the cafeteria didn't have anything to do with the fact Cassidy was going to call security on you if you didn't stop pacing like a caged animal?" She had just enough energy to smile, and Harvey seemed to go completely still.

His mouth turned up at the corners, sucking the oxygen from her chest. He had a dimple. To the right of his mouth, barely visible through the layers of beard growth, but it was there. She'd seen it. "That might've had something to do with it."

"Thank you." Drennan tried to sit higher in bed.

"I'll let your ob-gyn know you're awake and check back on you soon." Cassidy made herself scarce by dipping out another opening in the curtain, and the room suddenly felt so much smaller than a moment ago.

Harvey rounded the bed, taking up position on the stool her friend had vacated. "I wasn't sure what you liked, so I got a little bit of everything."

"I'll take chocolate-covered ants at this point, I'm so hungry." She grabbed both edges of the tray and settled it across her lap. He'd brought her a hamburger, some pasta, what looked like a tuna fish sandwich and a big fat slice of cheesecake. Her mouth watered at the sight of all those plump cherries in syrup he'd added. Yeah. She went for the cheesecake, almost willing to forgo manners and shove the entire thing in her mouth.

His laugh rumbled through the small space and notched her heart rate up higher, which registered on the stupid echocardiogram machine to her right. Great. She wasn't just splayed across this damn hospital bed—in one of the most vulnerable positions—but now her body's reactions would be loud enough for all to hear. "The cheesecake was actually for me."

Drennan paused with the fork heavy with that first bite halfway to her mouth. Disappointment lapped at her fragile steady state. A statement like that had once kicked her need for peace and survival into high alert. A past version of herself would've instantly dropped the fork and offered it back, but she'd earned this cheesecake, damn it. And she wanted it more than anything. "Don't you dare take food from a pregnant woman."

"Wouldn't dream of it." He settled back in the stool as easily as though it had a back support, crossing his feet at the ankles and his arms over his impressive chest. Harvey didn't say anything, simply studied her as though taking his eyes off her would hurt, and she...she didn't know what to do with that.

And she didn't want to know what he thought about having to come to her rescue. Didn't want to know if he regretted getting mixed up with her. He hadn't planned on getting involved in her life at all, still didn't want anything to do with her or the baby beyond financial obligation, and right then, she was sure he saw a woman so desperate for affection that she would seek it from someone who didn't even want friendship between them. And he wouldn't be wrong, would he?

"You don't have to be here." That first bite of creamy filling and the tart burst of cherries nearly dragged a moan from her throat, but the flood of sugar wasn't enough to drown out the chaotic self-deprecating thoughts. "I know you have other places you'd rather be."

"Dr. Yarrow called with an update on the victim we

pulled from the emerald pool. She was pregnant, a few weeks ahead of you." Drennan flinched as though he'd physically struck her. His voice dipped into dangerous territory, raising the hairs on the back of her neck. "So while I might have other places to be, Drennan, I'm not going anywhere."

Chapter Eighteen

"You didn't have to drive me home." Drennan shoved her key into the dead bolt slot and twisted the doorknob open. She walked straight into a too-small box that smelled of her. Something light and citrus, like a lemon orchard in the spring.

It drove deep into Harvey's lungs and set up residence in the fibers of his cells. Like she had over the course of the past few days. The hospital had given in to his demand to keep her overnight for observation, but there were limits on how long patients could remain in the ER. While he'd stepped out of the curtained section to give Drennan some privacy, the ob-gyn had assured them the baby hadn't suffered any damage from the abduction. Scanning the small box she called an apartment, Harvey memorized the layout. Living room front and center, the galley-style kitchen and dining space directly ahead, one bedroom off to the left. Probably with an attached bathroom. "What part of 'I'm not going anywhere' didn't you understand?"

"The part where you couldn't run fast enough in the other direction when I told you I was pregnant." She set her keys on the scratched black round dining table. The thing looked like it'd been spray-painted at one point, with natural wood scars peeking through. Worn at one edge where she most likely sat to eat every day. In fact, every piece of furniture in the place looked as though it'd been pulled straight from a dumpster or a thrift store, but all of it was clean. Odd. She'd been a trauma surgeon. She must've made good money before taking up a position as an assistant medical examiner. So either she preferred old furniture or she didn't have the funds to buy new. Maybe she didn't care.

He'd always been able to tell a lot by someone's home. What kind of person they were. Sentimental or functional, social or isolated, relationship focused or independent, habits, routines. Some things were harder to discern, and he was having a hell of a time holding himself back from asking the thousand questions on his mind. Like why she'd left a stable career to move into the middle of nowhere Utah to cut up dead people.

Knickknacks and books peppered the bookshelf set up on the other side of the TV, more books than personal trinkets. She was a reader, but Harvey had already known that. She was wicked intelligent with a medical background. A quick glimpse at the titles told him they were mostly crime thrillers and a handful of romances. All with cracks down their spines and flawed covers, to the point he was willing to bet these particular books were comfort reads. He found himself wondering which one would offer her some semblance of peace tonight.

"Yeah, well, things have changed, haven't they?" He couldn't explain the shift as he navigated around the once light sectional, the part of him that'd dreaded the idea of leaving her alone in that hospital bed. The man who'd abducted her had wilderness experience and used acronyms like a law enforcement official. This case... It was coming back on her. They'd both given a description of her abductor, but without the victim's identity, it would be hard to narrow down the man who'd killed her. He didn't like the statistics, but over 80 percent of women were killed by someone they knew. That was where they needed to start. If they were really lucky, the weapon he'd taken off her abductor would lead back to a name, but the State of Utah didn't require gun registration. Hell, if they could find something identifying the remains at the scene, they could get ahead of this, but the superintendent was ordering the Emerald Pools trail reopened despite the fact any evidence of their victim's death might be contaminated by the public. Drennan's gear had been left behind at the scene, but there'd been no sign of any of the victim's personal effects. Had the killer been there to get to them before she did?

But Drennan was right. He'd made his intentions concerning her and the baby clear, but that was before he'd learned someone had targeted her, and through her, his baby. That the son of a bitch had hurt her. "Besides, your doctor said I needed to keep an eye on you due to the hit you took to the back of your head."

"Of course she did." Drennan moved back into the living room, looking as antsy as he felt inside. He wasn't great at standing still. Being busy meant distracting himself from the buzz of thoughts he didn't want to take too close a look at. The military had been good for that. He'd been told when to eat, sleep and take a leak and where to be 24-7, and discharge had been a bigger shock than he'd expected. Folding her arms across her chest, she showed off the scrapes and bruises marring her forearms. "Well, I have a medical license. I think I am more than capable of taking care of myself."

Harvey studied her—really looked at her—recogniz-

ing that all-too-familiar pain in her eyes he'd gravitated
to the night they'd met, and his heart stuttered at the rawness. "You don't like it when other people try to take care
of you, do you?"

Her chin notched a few centimeters higher, her shoulders pulling back ever so slightly. It wasn't a big change
in her posture, but one he'd seen all the same. Like every
move she made tugged on some invisible connection between them and got him to pay closer attention. She bit
her bottom lip, hard enough that blood beaded quickly. "I
never said that."

He was moving before he consciously realized he'd
started closing the distance between them. "You didn't
have to. The second you woke up in my house yesterday,
you were trying to leave. Like your being there was some
great burden, even though I never gave you that impression.
It's more than not liking the attention, though, isn't it?"

He wasn't sure why he was pushing other than maybe
her answer might provide insight he'd been looking for
his entire life. Why, despite years of no contact and freedom and his father being buried six feet underground,
he couldn't seem to let go of the past. The one thing that
would free him, and the one thing that would damn him
at the same time.

Drennan didn't answer for a series of breaths. She didn't
have any reason to trust him, but he felt more than saw
the responding exhaustion filter into her expression. Like
she simply didn't have the energy to hide. "I don't want
to owe them anything, and I especially don't want to be
in debt to you."

"What makes you think you owe me anything?" Instinct had him closing those last few feet separating them.

"I didn't bring you back to my house or come after you in those woods to collect some kind of debt."

Her laugh surprised him, though it lacked the key ingredient of humor. "No. Just out of obligation, right?"

Harvey pulled up short. "Obligation?"

"Can you really tell me you would've done those things if I wasn't pregnant with your baby?" Her voice had lost some of its steadiness, the question a mere whisper to the emotion breaking her words. "Would you have stuck around the clinic both times if I hadn't told you? Would you be here now, making sure there's no one waiting in the apartment for me?"

He...he didn't know the answer to that. He knew what his father would've done, and hell, Harvey had gone out of his way to make sure he never followed in that bastard's footsteps. "I was attracted to you before you told me you were pregnant."

She pressed her lips together in a thin line. "That's not an answer, and, you know what? You don't owe me any kind of explanation or justification. I understand you can't help but want to protect your baby, really. But you asked why I can't stand the thought of someone else taking care of me? It's because admitting I need help or exposing what's important to me has always been used as a bargaining chip or to hold over my head, and I will never let someone have that kind of power over me again. Even the father of my child."

Harvey locked down the instant urge to argue with her logic, but he couldn't. She was right. He wouldn't have stayed at the clinic for any other woman he'd spent one night with. And he'd leave the search for her abductor to the law enforcement officers or Springdale police. But with Drennan... She brought out a protective streak he couldn't explain. He'd sworn not to put anyone's life in danger by getting close, but the baby connected them in a way he'd never expected to be linked to another human being. In less than forty-eight hours, it'd altered the very cells that made him who he was, had him doubting every decision he'd made up to this point in his life. That thought should've scared the crap out of him, but it didn't. Because in those hours where he'd imagined finding Drennan dead in those woods... Those had been the worst hours of his life. Hard as it was to admit to himself, losing her and the baby would've ripped him apart. "Why are you here, Drennan?"

Her name had never felt more right on his tongue, said like a prayer. Did she feel it? In the span of two days the woman had learned she was pregnant, passed out in the park, held her own against his stubborn ass and survived an abduction. She was strong, stronger than him. Fierce and ready to go toe to toe with anyone who dared talk down to her, but that kind of strength wasn't born. It was earned. "Why go from working as an emergency surgeon to a medical examiner in the middle of nowhere?"

Her throat worked on a swallow. Drennan took a step back, but she didn't make it far, her lower back connecting with one of her dining room chairs. "It's impossible to heal in the place you're being broken over and over."

Every muscle in his body tensed at the hurt in those words, at the fact that someone had taken this beautiful woman and been so careless. He wanted them to hurt just as much, if not more, to destroy them.

"It's hard to see the truth while you're stuck in the cycle." Drennan gazed at something over his shoulder, not really seeing him. "You're attached to people who have been distant with you. You're paying attention to people who ignore you. You make time for people who are too busy for you. You care about people who don't remember that you exist unless they need something. And even when you do whatever is asked of you, it's not enough. It's never enough, and it doesn't change anything. Years of wanting them to just…see you. Acknowledge that you're just as important to them as they are to you. You get your hopes up at the smallest hint of affection one minute, but then it's ripped right out from under you the next. Every time it breaks off something inside of you. Until there's nothing left. I was dying, and I didn't even know it. So I left."

Tears glistened in her eyes, and something simply *broke* inside of him. Because he'd been in that cycle, too, had watched his mother go through it countless times. Beatings one night and flowers the next. Fancy dinners for an anniversary followed up by a trip to the emergency room. Harvey had seen through the ploys to get him to cooperate, but his mom… She'd never had the chance. It was psychological warfare of the cruelest kind. And somehow Drennan had survived.

"That night at the bar, I just wanted to feel important to someone. To be someone's choice." Oh, hell. She hadn't wanted financial support for the baby from him. She'd wanted a real connection. She'd wanted someone to choose her for more than what she could do for them. Or the baby she carried. "And you offered me your hand with that charming smile, and I felt like the world wasn't burning around me anymore."

Harvey couldn't keep his distance anymore. Sliding his hands up her arms, he mapped the bruises and scrapes by touch, then tipped her chin enough to meet her gaze. "You're important to me, Drennan."

Her eyes snapped to his. "You're just saying that be-cause—"

"No. Not because of the baby. You." He shook his head, having his answer right then and there. He would've stayed in that clinic to make sure she was okay. He would've gone into those woods without a second thought to bring her back. "You changed me that night, Drennan. For the first time in years, I didn't want to be numb anymore."

He traced his thumb along her bottom lip, then devoured her mouth with his.

Chapter Nineteen

This kiss felt…different.

And that was a very bad thing.

A dangerous fire threatened to burst from beneath her skin as Harvey's mouth moved in a tantalizing rhythm over hers. She'd walked through some fires in her life, but this… She wasn't sure she could survive this. Right here, right now, nothing that'd happened between them existed. It was as though this was the first time, when all she could think about was that she wouldn't be able to take her next breath unless he touched her. All consuming, intense, insane.

Harvey kissed her like a man starved. Her mouth, down her neck, over her collarbone. His fingers threaded into her hair and pulled, arching her neck back for better access. Her lower back pressed into the dining room chair, but the pain never came. He didn't let it touch her as he slid one hand between her and the hardwood. He moved back to her mouth and kissed her. He kept on kissing her until Drennan feared she'd never recover from the deep, hot licks along the inside of her mouth. Her legs shook as her insides ached. He snaked his arm around her posterior rib cage, and it wasn't until then that she realized just how much bigger he was compared to her. That he could hurt her in a heartbeat.

But Harvey wouldn't ever hurt her.

He wasn't the man he feared becoming. That much was clear in the limited interactions they'd shared.

And she couldn't turn away from this. Drennan dug her fingernails into his back, most assuredly leaving marks, but she needed to get closer. To pull him into her. Because no matter how many times she reminded herself she'd done the right thing in giving herself up to her abductor in place of Dr. Yarrow or Harvey, she couldn't ignore the thick, oily terror that coated her insides. A shadow that pulsed with fear anytime Harvey got too far away. The killer had threatened her boss and the father of her child if he couldn't get what he wanted from her. But, here, in his arms, those threats couldn't dig its claws in as deep. With him, she could forget about the way her abductor had looked at her as though she was nothing more than a means to an end. She could forget that same look on her mother's face and the pure vitriol saved in the form of voicemails on her phone.

Harvey framed one hand against her jaw, smoothing his thumb along the curve and down the front of her throat. His breathing had reached chaotic levels—matching hers—and she liked it. She liked that she'd had this effect on him, that of everything he'd survived, everything he'd been through and done, she had the power to push him to his limits. "Bedroom."

Drennan could only nod as he pulled her back against his chest, his mouth seeking hers once more. They walked as one, him backing toward her bedroom door, her too out of her mind to warn him to watch out for the corner of the photograph she'd hung only a couple weeks ago.

His shoulder skimmed the frame and sent it rocking then to the floor. Plastic, a generic photograph of flowers and brushed metal warped, taking out a chunk of one of the baseboards on impact. Hands gripped on her waist, Harvey didn't break his hold as he helped her maneuver around the mess. "I can fix that."

"I don't care." She'd gone too long without his mouth on hers. He could destroy every single piece of furniture in this place and she wouldn't bat an eye as long as she could hold on to this feeling. Hold on to him. For however long he gave her. Maybe just tonight. Maybe longer. Because she believed him after she'd told him about the pregnancy. Harvey didn't want to be a father. His past had contorted the meaning into something perverse and threatening, and there was nothing she could say to rewrite that innate belief he held on to. He wouldn't let himself get close to anyone. She didn't question that, she'd seen that fear in his expression. So she would have this. She'd live in the now, stop trying to shape the future and remind herself she wasn't responsible for making other people happy as she'd been taught nearly her whole life. His fingertips dug into the soft curve of her hips, and Drennan arched into him. "Please."

She didn't know what she was begging for. Only that he was the only one who could meet the out-of-control need.

Guiding her over the threshold of her bedroom door, Harvey swung her around, easing her onto the bed. Gaze locked on her. He swept his fingers over her face and set a strand of hair behind her ear. "You're beautiful, you know that? You're strong and patient and you give a damn about other people." His voice lowered to a whisper. "If anyone is having my baby, I'm glad it's you."

Unfiltered heat seared through her veins. She couldn't remember the last time someone had complimented her. It seemed like an easy thing, but Harvey proved his earlier point when he looked at her like this. Like she was important. "You're just saying that to get me back into bed."

His laugh charged through him. The effect lit up something inside of her she hadn't allowed herself to feel in years, something bright and breathtaking and light. Harvey twisted his head to one side, setting his temple against her chin, then shifted his weight into his elbows on either side of her head. "You know me so well, but as much as I'm looking forward to a second time around with you, you should rest."

Threading her fingers into his hair, Drennan knew he was right. She'd survived her initial abduction, but the hit to her head would likely trigger side effects if she overdid it. Not to mention the drain of growing an entire human being. But his weight had settled more of that oily terror trying to bubble its way to the surface, and she wasn't ready to let that go. She skimmed her fingertips over his jaw, through his beard and back, memorizing everything she could about this moment. Where they were just Drennan and Harvey. No homicide, no victim, no jobs or past. Two people who had somehow found a way to each other, where the outside world didn't exist and there were no expectations. "Will you stay with me?"

"I told you I'm not going anywhere." Harvey slid down her front toward the end of the bed. "Get some sleep, Drennan. I'll keep you safe."

She tightened her hold on him, and Harvey seemed to freeze under her touch. "Here. Stay here. With me. Please."

He didn't move, didn't even breathe as far as she could tell. One second. Two. He was going to do the right thing. He was going to tell her sleeping in the same bed wasn't a good idea, and the disappointment would hurt, but she would pretend it didn't. She'd survived worse, right? Harvey slipped one hand along her rib cage. "Yeah. I can stay if that will make you feel better."

It would. More than he'd ever know, but she'd keep that small slice of truth to herself. Navigating farther up the bed, Drennan sank into the pillows, suddenly more exhausted as desire drained. Her eyes grew heavy, each blink becoming harder to get through. "Thank you."

"You don't have to thank me for that." Strong fingers curved around her ankle as he pulled one of her shoes off and dropped it to the floor, then the other. The act was simple enough but meant the world.

Nobody cooked for her. Nobody cleaned for her. Nobody made her meals or did her laundry. Nobody from her past life had reached out to check in, to make sure she was okay. Nobody catered to her, period, she was always the one others relied on to help them through. Her entire life, she'd stepped up to take care of everyone else, even dedicated her entire adult life to helping others as a trauma surgeon, in hopes just one person—someone, *anyone*— would return the favor. That step had slowly become an expectation, then a demand. But she'd held on to that hope. Days. Months. Years. Until it'd finally been crushed from her very being.

Except now Harvey had set his hand on her hip, rolling her onto her front so he could drag the blankets out from underneath her and settle them over her frame. The bed dipped with his added weight as he maneuvered in behind her, his front pressed against her back, and her entire body stiffened at the prospect of falling asleep with someone else beside her. She'd never done that before. Past boyfriends hadn't minded. They latched on to the casual emotional distance she'd kept between them, because sixty-hour workweeks didn't allow for anything more. But the heat sinking through her bruised skin now—Harvey's body heat—and into the dull aches and sore muscles, felt better than she'd ever expected. Like slipping into a warm bath or getting lost in her favorite comfort read. It felt like being at home. Soft and familiar and safe.

"Is this okay?" Harvey's exhales skimmed over the back of her neck. Shifting, he slipped one hand over her hip, then flat against her belly. Over where their baby grew. His other arm wedged beneath her pillow, caging her against him, but this cage wasn't meant to trap her.

Unable to form a single answer, Drennan nodded. They'd been intimate together. Hell, they'd conceived a baby together, however accidentally, but this...this superseded casual. This was *more*, and that was a very dangerous place to be. Because she wanted more. With him, for them. She wanted the family dinners and the trips into Zion with the baby strapped to his back. She wanted the ice cream weekends and petty arguments about money and where to go on vacation. For the first time in longer than she cared to admit, she *wanted*. Enough that the realization sucked the breath straight out of her lungs. But the shock that really threatened to unease her? She was allowed to want. There wasn't anyone who would stop her. No one to guilt her into giving up that dream that would take her from that neat little nurturer package she'd become over the years. No one to shame her for daring to imagine a different life. She was free to want Harvey, to want a family of her own.

"You okay?" His thumb circled around her belly button. Once. Twice. She lost count of the passes he made, starting small then spreading out wider until he brushed the edge of her waistband beneath her scrubs top. "You should get some sleep."

She wanted to, more than anything after what she'd survived, but her brain refused to stop spiraling. Every pass of his fingers over the sensitive skin of her belly brought her back to what he'd revealed in the ER. "She was pregnant."

Harvey's fingers stilled. Just for a moment. And that hesitation rattled her deep into her bones. "Yeah. She was."

"Do you think that's why he killed her?" Her voice shook without her permission. "That it was some kind of affair gone wrong?"

Seconds ticked by. Then a minute. She wasn't sure Harvey would answer, and she knew why. Neither of them wanted to imagine two lives ended prematurely by something they were currently working through. It was too real. Too…close to reality, considering his fear of becoming the man who'd ultimately killed his mother. His thumb made another pass around her navel, soothing her nerves, and he seemed to relax muscle by muscle.

"I'm not sure, but I need you to know I'm not going to let anything happen to you." The hand braced under the pillow curled around, threading through her hair and pulling it away from her face. His lips pressed into the hyperaware skin below her ear, the combination of his hands and his mouth dragging her into unconsciousness. "I'm not giving you up that easily."

Chapter Twenty

His body felt heavier than ever before. At…peace.

Harvey blinked against the sunlight coming through the window to his right. Cream linen curtains shifted as the vent puffed out cool air. Plants had been hung in the corner nearest him, the aesthetic natural and calming compared to the chaos outside these walls. Not his room. Not his house. This was… He was with Drennan. Her apartment. Hell, he'd fallen asleep. His chest worked against the weight pressing against him, but he didn't dare move.

Drennan had turned into him sometime during the night, her head nestled against his heart, seeking him out even in unconsciousness. Scraped fingers and broken nails rested over his stomach, with one of her legs thrown over his, pinning him in place. Holding on to him as though she couldn't stand the thought of losing him. She fit so perfectly. Harvey lifted her fingers up, rubbing dried blood from her nails. Law enforcement had gathered what they could of her clothing and evidence from under her nails after the abduction—but the sight of so much damage squeezed his heart.

She was innocent. Maybe simply in the wrong place at the wrong time. Had Dr. Yarrow or he been there in her place to collect the victim's personal items from the pond, it's possible she never would've been taken. Because the alternative meant someone had targeted her, would keep coming for her any chance they got, until they succeeded in whatever plan they'd concocted. Her fingers curled into his, grabbing tight. A soft hitch in her breath kicked his heart rate up. Damn, she was beautiful like this. Without the stress of the past, the pressure of survival and the paleness of creating life in sleep, her face had softened, and a similar ease filtered through him.

He hadn't slept as well as he had last night in…ever. Every noise, every change in his surroundings had potentially been a threat, whether at home or in the military. Survival had trained him to sleep light. Even then, no more than a few hours at a time, but with Drennan here, he'd found something he'd never imagined. Peace. It echoed through his limbs, made him feel heavier, grounded and sluggish. Her body heat seeped past his clothing and soothed his frayed nervous system.

Harvey scanned her bedroom, then the living room through the open door. There was only one access into her second-floor apartment, but the security in this building wasn't strong enough to stop someone from getting in if they put their mind to it. The locks on the windows were cheap, the front door only secured by a dead bolt that could be bypassed by taking out the too-small hinges on the other side of the door. One kick and the entire thing would collapse. Which meant Drennan was still possibly in danger. That his—*their*—baby was in danger.

Setting her hand back against his chest, he counted off her breaths, and the manic concern that'd set up residence over the past couple of days died down. In. Out. Slow. Controlled. He couldn't think of a single stimulus that'd unwound years of physical and mental tension the way her breathing did, but Harvey knew it wasn't just that. It was her. For some unknown reason, she felt safe enough to ask him to stay last night, to seek him out. She...trusted him. Him. A man who couldn't even trust himself, who fought an invisible battle each and every day to keep himself level and from falling into a darkness he'd never escape once he got a taste. And given her past, he understood what a gift that trust was.

To be someone's choice.

Her words had gutted him faster than the KA-BAR knife he'd failed to dodge in Afghanistan. Drennan had never felt important to anyone, and he hadn't lied. She'd become important to him. Not just because of the baby. Long before that, when every cell in his body had argued against letting her walk out his door the night they'd met. And, hell, she deserved someone who would do whatever it took to keep her happy and satisfied. Who could bring out that smile without even trying. Someone she trusted not to use her up and spit her out. Who made her feel important day in and day out.

His chest rose on a deep inhale as he stared up at the ceiling. He could be that. He could choose her and wake up to Drennan clinging to him as though she couldn't breathe without him every morning. He could surprise her with her favorite takeout and spend the night with her legs wrapped around his waist. He could taste her skin and draw that breathy little moan from her lips every night after they put the baby down for bed. He could prove she was important, that she was worth a lifetime of dedication and care. They could be something more than two people tied by the small life they'd created.

If he could trust himself.

His temperature spiked, Drennan's body heat suddenly

too much to handle despite her thin scrubs and the fact they'd lost the blanket sometime in the middle of the night. His heart rate notched higher as he fought the urge to dig his fingers into her arm to hold on to that peaceful feeling for a little while longer. But that invisible demon that'd been passed down in his DNA had already opened one eye and started watching him. Daring him to make a move, to shove her off just so he could breathe a little easier. To give him a reason to attack.

And that was how he would spend the rest of his life.

On the defense. Constantly on alert. Waiting for her or the baby to trigger him into overreacting. To the point all the nightmares he'd suffered over the years became reality. Because no matter how well he'd slept last night or how often he reveled in these too-short moments of peace, Drennan wasn't capable of slaying demons. And she shouldn't have to destroy her life trying. Hoping. He… couldn't put her through that. Couldn't put anyone through that.

"Mmm. Sorry. I didn't realize I was using you as a pillow." She turned her face into his chest, breathing him in as she fisted his T-shirt, and Harvey froze. Her smile lit up her whole face as she blinked up at him and rolled onto her back. With her head on his arm—long asleep from her weight now—she pointed her toes in an exaggerated stretch, showing off all the sweet curves. In a couple months, she'd have one more as the baby got bigger, and something primal inside of him wanted to watch every step of the change. To feel the baby kick and move, watch him or her react to the different kinds of foods Drennan ate. He wanted to rub her feet when the swelling started and make those late-night grocery runs for whatever she was craving. He wanted it all. And he couldn't have it. Couldn't have her. Her eyes cleared of sleep as she turned back into him. "You do make a good pillow, though."

His laugh shuddered through him, easy and quick. When was the last time he'd really laughed like that? He couldn't remember. But with Drennan, it was becoming easier. "You don't. You're all skin and bones."

"Hey. There used to be some curves here." The feigned seriousness in her expression charged another laugh he couldn't stop even if he'd wanted to. Drennan slipped her hand across his chest, seemingly memorizing him as much as he'd memorized her. "Our baby stole them all. It's not my fault it doesn't like anything I put in my mouth."

His smile slipped.

Their baby. Harvey swallowed the knot of dryness in his throat. She still considered the baby to be theirs. Not just hers. And that...that couldn't happen. Tension bled into his shoulders as he extracted himself from the tangle of limbs and bedding that smelled just as he remembered. No. Better. His clothing stuck to his spine.

"Want some breakfast?" She'd rolled onto her side, watching him as he went for his boots, one fist propped along her jaw. The circles under her eyes had lightened, giving her a brighter appearance. "I haven't really been shopping the past couple of weeks, but I think I have a few eggs and some bacon in the fridge."

"No. Thanks." A hum of warning had started under his skin, urging him to get as far from Drennan as possible. He'd let this get too far. One-night stands weren't supposed to be anything more, and he'd broken his own damn rule by agreeing to stay in bed with her last night. He'd known better than to allow himself to want something more, but he was better than his father. He could do the right thing.

Harvey shoved his feet into his boots and tied them as quickly as he could. "I need to get going."

Disappointment washed over her face as she sat up, her voice softer than he'd ever heard it before. The bruises on her face—where the son of a bitch who'd taken her dared put his hands on her—had darkened into a mottled black-and-blue Rorschach pattern he'd never be able to unsee. It hadn't been his hands that'd hurt her, but it was all too easy for his brain to conjure images just like this down the line. Not happening. Ever. Because he would leave. He'd put as much distance between them as possible if that was what would keep her and the baby safe, but the portion of his soul that'd found a sliver of calm in this apartment protested leaving her like this.

"What are you doing, Harvey?"

"I have a shift in the park." He didn't, but he needed to check in with Ranger Simpson. See if anything was found at the bottom of the upper emerald pool that could help identify their victim or tell them who might've killed her. He also wanted to know if a name had been attached to that gun. In revealing the victim's pregnancy, Dr. Yarrow had provided them with a possible motive behind her death, but it wasn't enough. Without an ID, they had no suspect unless the samples taken from Drennan came back with DNA evidence. And considering she'd been knocked unconscious and fallen into the pool, he wasn't hanging all of his hopes on forensics.

"Oh. Okay. In that case, I guess I should check in with Dr. Yarrow." Running one hand down her face, she grabbed for her phone on the nightstand. "See if anything more has come through from the autopsy or if he needs me to go back to the scene."

"You're not going anywhere near the scene. You should

ask Dr. Yarrow to give you a few days off. He called with an update last night." Harvey searched for his jacket. He didn't remember taking it off in the living room, but it wasn't in here, and Drennan's scent was starting to drive him crazy, urging him to get back into that bed and breathe it in until it became part of him. "Let him take point on the autopsy and the investigation for now. You shouldn't have to do anything but recover."

Her gaze snapped to his, her thumb hovering over the screen of her phone. "Why would you even think to say that?"

Harvey straightened. "Because you were knocked unconscious, nearly drowned, abducted and tied to a tree yesterday. Not to mention you've been throwing up everything you eat and passed out from dehydration the day before. You're not in a position to go back to work."

"And you're not in a position to make those kinds of decisions for me. I can still do my job." A hardness slipped over her face. Drennan became unnaturally still, and for the first time since they'd met, he thought he might be looking at the woman who'd learned to endure years of mental and emotional abuse by shutting herself down. Becoming nothing and no one to survive. "I...need to see this through."

"Not happening." He took a step toward her. "Not when you're barely able to stand and not when the man who abducted you is still out there."

Her phone pinged with an incoming message, tearing her attention from him, and a release swept through his chest. As though he'd been holding his breath, waiting for the woman he knew to come back to him. "The dental records I requested for the woman found in Emerald Pools came back positive." She lifted the phone before tossing it on the bed, that hard layer of emotionless armor still in place. "We have an ID."

Chapter Twenty-One

Ellender Garza.

The dark-haired woman Drennan had collected from the Emerald Pools trail finally had a name. It would take more than that to discern who could've ended her life, but it was a start. The background check the law enforcement rangers had run told her the victim was only in her early thirties. Never married, employed by Springdale's very own mayor as an assistant for the past several years. She didn't have any large debts or a mortgage that might've gotten her in trouble, and a quick review of her social media accounts hadn't pinpointed any kind of boyfriend who might've been the father of her child. Her parents had passed years before, leaving their victim everything, including her childhood home and two vehicles, one of which was recovered in the visitor's center parking lot once they had the license and registration info. The rangers were searching the vehicle and had brought Springdale PD in to search her home, but as far as Drennan could tell, Ellender Garza was very much an average woman who probably hadn't meant to get pregnant.

Like her.

Hot water coasted down her body as she rinsed shampoo from her hair. Stinging needles pricked at her scalp as the soap made contact with the sensitive skin around the stitches. It didn't matter how many times she'd scrubbed herself from head to toe, she could still feel her abductor's grip around her arms, feel him tightening the rope at her wrists. Taste the scummy water of the pond. She'd fought back, but it hadn't been enough. He'd left bruises on more than her skin. They were etched onto her soul now.

But she thought they might not have ached as much when she'd fallen asleep with Harvey's fingers drawing circles around her navel last night and his hand in her hair. Or when she'd woken in his arms this morning. Having him in bed with her—just holding her—had eased the pressure in her chest and fought back the nightmares that usually came. Dreams her brain conjured showing her exactly what she'd never have. Her parents, happy, healthy and alive, doing random, everyday things like getting into arguments about where to eat for dinner or visiting her long-since-passed grandmother. Most people would consider images like that as anything but a nightmare, but every time they came, her heart broke a little more. What else would she call them?

But she remembered her dream from last night. She'd woken up to it this morning. Real and warm and within arm's reach. Literally. Except something had changed. Regret had infiltrated Harvey's voice, his expression and his body language. He hadn't said it in as many words, but it'd been there. In the way he'd extracted himself from her bed, how he'd rushed to leave. He'd made a mistake. That much she could see of the few minutes they'd had together, and she'd known it'd been coming. She just hadn't expected to be so…hollow. But she wouldn't beg. She wouldn't try to convince him to see her worthy of the risk of getting close to someone. She'd spent far too many years asking people to love her, and not a single one had ended in her favor. She wouldn't put herself through that again, no matter how much she wished Harvey could see himself as she saw him.

As devoted and aware, to the point he understood exactly what was needed in any given moment. As intriguing and discerning of who he allowed into his life, as she'd failed to be so many times in hers. Curious and impressive in every way that counted. Kind, brave, responsible. He'd told her she was strong, that she was important, but didn't he see the same attributes in himself?

Another slap of pain arched across her scalp, and Drennan turned off the water. Her skin had pinkened just under blistering from the temperature of the water and the amount of times she'd scrubbed herself clean, and already she wanted to climb back into the shower. She wouldn't. She didn't care what Harvey thought she should tell Dr. Yarrow. She needed to get to the office to help the ME finish out the autopsy and provide law enforcement as many details about Ellender Garza as possible. She needed to see this investigation through. Drennan grabbed for the towel she'd left on the toilet seat and stepped in front of the fogged mirror while drying.

Her lower belly looked as it always did as she dragged the terry cloth across her midsection. No signs of showing yet, but within the next few of weeks, her pants would fit tighter and she'd have no choice but to shop for maternity clothes. Had Ellender Garza started showing? According to Harvey, she'd been a few weeks ahead of Drennan's pregnancy, but it'd been hard to tell with the amount of bloat given off by the bacteria in her body breaking down upon death.

The on call ob-gyn had been rerouted for an emergency

delivery during the ultrasound to check on the baby. Drennan and Harvey had left the hospital with assurances everything was okay with the pregnancy, and she'd been too tired and beaten to let the anxiety win. But what if the doctor had been wrong? What if something had been missed? Now she'd had at least eight hours of sleep, a shower and soon an entire plate of breakfast food. Her head was clear, and the spiraling thoughts were at full force. The friends from her previous life—including Cassidy—had all been career-focused women putting off having families until their practices were established. She didn't have experience with what was normal or abnormal in a pregnancy, and the one person who might be able to help her through wasn't in a position to do anything for anyone but herself. Ellender Garza might've seen an ob-gyn once she found out she was pregnant. Maybe even the same doctor Cassidy had recommended to Drennan. She would've gotten to hear the heartbeat of her baby and see the sonograms of the little gray-and-white outline growing week by week. She would've had questions and gotten answers and wondered if eating sushi really wasn't allowed.

But someone had taken that from her.

Cut her life short, her baby's life short.

And Drennan had come so close to the same end. That was why she had to see this through, why she'd run herself into the ground if it meant getting justice for those two souls. Ellender Garza hadn't deserved her death. So Drennan would make sure her killer paid the price.

"We're going to be okay, right?" Turning to one side, she slipped her hand over the spot where the baby would round out. Harvey was right. She was skin and bones, the impressions of her ribs peeking through her skin. She'd have to move to a high-fat diet full of peanut butter and avocados if she couldn't keep anything down soon.

Securing the towel beneath her arms, she wrenched the bathroom door open. And saw Harvey. She sucked in a lungful of air as he stood on the other side of the bed, his phone in hand. "Oh. I... I didn't think you were still here."

Her skin flushed with the awareness that all that separated them was a bath towel and her queen-size bed. Honestly, she wasn't sure how they'd fit together so well last night with his broad chest and ability to take up an entire room with his intensity. Drennan clutched the towel harder at the memory of his body pressed against hers, his knee wedged between her legs, how he'd held on to her hip and dragged her closer. His agreement to stay with her might not have sounded like much, but it was everything to her.

"What are these?" His cheeks seemed to sink in, carving out deeper shadows running the length of his jaw and under his eyes. "All these messages from an unknown number."

"Wait. Is that my phone?" Fury replaced the tendrils of appreciation and desire. She took a step forward to grab it from him from over the bed, but Harvey easily dodged her attempt. "You had no right to read through my private messages. Give it to me."

She felt like a five-year-old whining for her favorite toy.

His gaze locked on her. Hard and cold and a little bit terrifying. "First of all, you left it unlocked on the bed so I could read the dental results. Our victim's name is Ellender Garza. I sent that information on to the law enforcement rangers so they can start pulling a victim profile together. Second, I didn't mean to read through your messages. A new message came through while I was reading the results that started with the words, 'You've always been a selfish brat.' So yeah, I clicked on it to make sure it was coming from a wrong number, and I didn't have to pay someone a visit."

Her body locked up on her. Her mind went blank. No. No, no, no. This wasn't part of the deal. Reality wasn't supposed to breach the bubble they'd created in this room. In here, they were just two people who cared about each other and happened to be having a baby together. No talk of the past or the future or the threat outside these walls. Drennan closed her eyes against the shame charging through her. Those messages… She'd kept them and all the voicemails as a reminder not to trust the upward arc of the cycle where her mother said what Drennan wanted to hear and pretended to give a damn. To force herself to see the truth. No one was ever supposed to see them, least of all him.

Harvey tossed the phone on the bed, face up. Full of messages just like that one from her mother. He pointed down at the phone. "Except there are countless others just like that one from that specific number, spanning months. Who the hell has been messaging you that vile crap, and where can I find them, Drennan?"

She didn't know what to say, couldn't remember how to breathe.

"Is this the person you won't tell me about?" He was right there, suddenly standing in front of her. She hadn't heard him move, or maybe she'd been too wrapped up in her own thoughts to track him rounding the end of the bed and coming to stand in front of her. His thumb traced the bottom edge of her lip, so light she could've imagined it. "The one who hurt you? Who is it?"

Tears burned in her eyes. She'd tried. She'd tried to hide it, to not blame herself for all the accusations and disappointment thrown her way, but abuse—in any form—liked to be kept a secret. That was where it did the most damage, isolated its victims and crushed all sources of hope. It'd built until she couldn't handle the pressure anymore, and the control she'd convinced herself was enough broke. Her mouth wobbled the harder she attempted to hold it in. "My dad died when I was eight. It was a car accident. The kind most people don't walk away from, but I did."

Harvey pulled back slightly, but not out of reach. "I'm sorry."

"So am I. He was my best friend. No matter how tired he was at the end of a long workday at the hospital or what else needed to be done, he went out of his way to spend time with me every day." A smile tugged at her mouth, but even she could feel it didn't last long as the grief rolled in. Not as strong as it used to but still there. She wasn't sure she'd ever stop feeling it. "We did everything together as a family. Just him, me and my mom. They were the perfect couple. Teasing each other while they made dinner together, laughing at inside jokes, sneaking kisses when they thought I couldn't see, but after he died, my mom changed. It was like a switch had been flipped. There weren't any more trips to the nearest gas station for a treat or sitting down to dinner together. Her smiles were gone, and I couldn't figure out why she would get this look on her face anytime she saw me. Like I was a stranger."

Straightening to his full height, Harvey gave her a glimpse of the soldier she knew him to be. Alert, ready. "Your dad was a doctor?"

Her heart squeezed too hard in her chest. She nodded. "I thought I could make her proud by following in his footsteps, but she didn't see it that way."

"She took her grief out on you, a child who was grieving her father as much as she was grieving her husband."

He lost that hardness as he stepped into her, his knuckles grazing her cheek. The touch elicited a whole new sensation in her chest, as though she suddenly had room to feel something more than the armor she'd built against the people in her life. "And she still is, isn't she?"

"No. Because I won't let her. She sends me messages and leaves voicemails, but I never respond back. I don't answer her calls." She'd never spoken about any of this. Cassidy had been witness to her mother's confrontations in the middle of the ER when she felt she wasn't getting enough attention, but right now, Drennan wanted this to last longer. This…unloading. Where she peeled back another layer of the empty, compliant outlet she'd been nearly her whole life and exposed the woman she knew herself to be underneath. She wanted him to be part of that. She wanted to delay the inevitable moment Harvey realized he'd started caring about her more than he set out to, about what happened to her and the baby. That moment was coming, and there was nothing she could do to stop it, but she could push it off a little while longer. With moments like this. "I took away her power over me, and she's desperate to get it back."

The notches between his eyebrows deepened. Did he know he was still touching her as though he needed that connection between them? "So then why keep them?"

"To remind myself I am not the abuse I endured." Another invisible layer peeled back, revealing a spark of something she'd felt the night they'd met. "I'm the hope that refused to surrender."

Chapter Twenty-Two

She wasn't the abuse she endured.

A resounding echo thudded hard in Harvey's chest.

"No more, Drennan." He turned for the bed, collecting her phone from the comforter that had kept them tangled together throughout the night. He handed the device off. The choice was entirely up to her. He couldn't make it for her. "Stop putting yourself in a position to get hurt. You have good intentions in reminding yourself of what she's capable of, but one of these days, a message will come through that won't do that job. It will do what she intends, and you'll be right back to being her metaphorical punching bag."

She sighed. "I know. I've told myself to block and delete her number so many times." Tears glittered in her eyes. She nodded, as though trying to convince herself—of recognizing—that what he said made sense. "I just keep hoping she'll realize her mistake and she'll remember that I'm her daughter. That she's supposed to love me."

He didn't know the specifics of what her mother had put her through, but he couldn't help but admire the woman who'd come out on the other side of it. How Drennan had stood there and braved exposing a piece of herself she'd guarded for so long. Because he knew she had. He knew the lengths she'd gone through to protect her abuser out of shame and potential disbelief from people who were supposed to care about her. He'd done the exact same thing. Lying to his teachers, pushing away his friends, not making eye contact with anyone long enough for them to realize the bruises on his face hadn't come from falling down the stairs the second time in a week. He'd isolated himself just to avoid having to answer questions about his home life and ensuring his father's wrath if the man ever found out about it. It hadn't gotten any easier in the military, but at least he hadn't been—how had Drennan put it?—trying to heal in the same place he'd been broken.

And Drennan was... She was awe-inspiring. Stronger than anyone he'd ever known, including the men and women in his unit, and everything he wasn't. She'd overcome that part of her that relived every injury and harsh word over and over to get her through the day. He wanted that. More than anything he wanted to move past the hollowness in his chest and find something worth reaching out for. But the man he'd become had been built on years of detachment, grief and pain, and letting go felt like forgiving. Something he wasn't sure he could ever bring himself to do.

He stepped into her, drawn by more than the need to offer some semblance of comfort—if he was capable of that at all. He wanted to feel her, breathe her in, make her and the peace she brought part of him. Harvey pressed a soft kiss to her mouth, excited by her gasp, as he shifted her damp hair away from her face. "People like your mother will always need someone to blame. They teach you that love is not unconditional or deserved, that it's given only when certain expectations and whims are met. They need the control and use manipulation to feel powerful, and when you don't give them what they want or you fight back, you become the villain. But, Drennan, I would much rather see you as the villain in her story than as a victim."

She swiped at her face. "I don't want to be a victim. I want to be the mother this baby needs."

Hell, that threatened to gut him on the spot. She was one of the few, the ones who recognized the cycle and refused to pass it along to the next generation. If his father had been brave enough to make that choice... Harvey didn't know where he would be. "You already are."

Her laugh punctured through the hard layer of ice he'd set in his chest. Clear and full of a brightness he hadn't let himself recognize in a long time. "You don't have to say that. I'm sure all of this is too much to handle, even for you."

"I can handle you." He kissed her again, this one more than an offer of comfort. The sweep of his tongue was driven by the need to reward her for all the hard days, the lonely nights and the tears she'd shed for a woman who didn't deserve a single one of them.

"You should get dressed." Harvey skimmed his knuckles along her throat, reveling in the strong beat of her pulse. Warmth radiated into his hand at the contact, and he wanted to drown in it. To drag her back into that bed and help them both forget the atrocities they'd survived. That was what they were. That was what the pain in her eyes that'd called to him the night they'd met spoke of. Survival. It was something they shared, something that bonded them, but every cell in his body told him even without that, he'd still feel this unexplainable connection to get close to her. He fanned his fingers over her jaw, framing one side of her face. "I want to drop by the clinic to get you that ultrasound before I head into the park to follow up with the law enforcement rangers. Make sure everything is okay with the baby."

"I'll just need a few minutes." Nodding, Drennan clutched at the towel with a wisp of a smile as she backed toward the bathroom door. "Thank you."

A swell of something foreign climbed his throat, but he wouldn't let it out. Nothing he said in response would be worthy of the woman having his baby, so Harvey sat back on the edge of the mattress to wait. No one had ever thanked him for his advice, but then again, he'd never felt comfortable giving it. While he might've gone through his own personal hell, he'd kept that part of his life locked up tight. But it'd felt good to talk Drennan through those contradictory feelings of wanting to destroy the threat to your well-being while trying to make it love you at the same time. Felt freeing. Healing. True to her word, mere minutes passed before she stepped back into the bedroom clothed in black slacks and a T-shirt and tennis shoes and they were on their way to the clinic.

Harvey maneuvered into the parking lot he was becoming all too familiar with and rounded the front of the SUV to help Drennan out. Based on her hesitation and automatic reaching for the door, he was betting no one had done that for her, either. Or she hadn't let them, needing to prove she could make it through this life without help. He understood that. Didn't mean he was going to let her.

The nurses at the front desk welcomed Drennan with a smile while side-eyeing him at the same time. Couldn't blame them. The last two times he'd been here, he'd nearly brought the entire building down with his demands for them to prioritize Drennan. It'd been selfish considering all the people—young, old and somewhere in the middle— waiting their turn, but he didn't regret a single moment.

He hadn't lied to her before. She was important. Maybe the most important person in his life.

Another shard of ice cracked from inside his chest, breaking off into nothingness as though it'd never existed. That...that wasn't supposed to happen. She wasn't supposed to be important. He wasn't supposed to want more of her in his life. Harvey stilled as a nurse led Drennan back into the corridor with private rooms branching off each side.

She turned toward him with a smile. "They're ready for us."

"You go on. You don't want me in there." His voice remained steady despite the storm building inside. Harvey flexed both hands at his sides, trying to get the feeling back into them. "I'll wait."

"I thought you wanted to make sure the baby was okay." The divots between her brows deepened as she studied him. He did, and he wanted nothing more than her to have this. The experience of hearing the baby's heartbeat after everything she'd been through in those woods. Of seeing their child on the ultrasound screen, healthy and unharmed. It wouldn't relieve all the anxiety and stress she held on to, but it would go a long way to ensuring she had a healthy pregnancy, and Drennan deserved his support. She closed the distance between them, lowering her voice. "I know this probably isn't how you imagined our situation going, but I'm not sure I can do this on my own. Please."

Oh, hell. Blood drained from his face. She was scared of getting bad news. Of being alone when it happened. And he'd... Damn it. He was being a selfish bastard. Harvey nodded. More to himself than her. "Yeah. Of course."

He kept to her side as they followed on the nurse's heels. Drennan stepped on a scale outside of another nurses' station and was led into one of the private rooms where the nurse took her blood pressure and monitored her oxygen levels. "Is this all normal?"

"Yep. We just want to make sure Mom is taking care of herself before we check on baby." The nurse rolled around on her stool, peeling the blood pressure cuff from Drennan's arm before leading her to the exam table. "It's all routine. Nothing to worry about, Daddy."

Daddy. He was going to be a dad in seven months, whether he wanted this or not. A tingling set up in his fingers as he clutched on to the chair arms.

"Go ahead and lay back, Mom. Pull up your shirt and unbutton your pants." The nurse grabbed a condiment bottle with a long nozzle from the cart holding the ultrasound equipment. "Don't want to get any of the jelly on your clothes. It's gonna be a little cold at first."

Drennan followed instructions as though she'd done this a thousand times before. As a physician, he imagined she'd seen it done many times, but living it and observing it were two different things. Her fingers shook as she tried to unbutton her slacks. She was still nervous, and Harvey's instincts kicked in.

"I got it." Shooting to his feet, he set his hand over both of hers and made quick work of the button and zipper before interlacing one hand into hers. The act itself didn't even come close to what they'd shared in making this baby, but the floor threatened to sweep out from under him, anyway.

"All right. Let's see how baby is doing." The nurse took up her rolling stool and detached a wand-looking device from the cart. She pressed it larger side down onto Drennan's stomach, then smoothed it over the jelly.

A rapid *thud thud thud* filled the room. Fast and almost

out of control. Drennan's hand squeezed around his and refused to let go.

"There's baby's heartbeat." The nurse shifted the device around. "Nice and strong."

"That's good." Tangible relief drained from Drennan's shoulders as she stared at the monitor. She collapsed back against the exam table, her free hand pressed to her forehead. The tears she'd held in earlier escaped down the sides of her face, and he couldn't help but try to catch them before they made it to her hair.

"Strong heartbeat." He didn't know what else to say that might keep her concern at bay.

"Yeah." She swiped at her face and sat up again. "I'm so glad."

He couldn't make anything out but a bunch of gray and white clouds across the black background, but then... There it was. The thud matched up with a flutter on the screen, and Harvey's chest nearly exploded from holding his breath. An outline materialized with another shift of the ultrasound wand. Baby-shaped and very real.

Their baby.

His baby.

"I've spent so long dreaming of this moment." A smile broke across Drennan's face as she stared at the monitor then turned her attention to him. "Thank you."

The tingling flared from his fingers into his arms and then his chest. It woke that monster living in his blood like a predator latching on to the scent of its prey, and Harvey felt his body temperature drop. He hadn't heard her right. "What did you just say?"

"Harvey?" Drennan's voice failed to bring the peace it usually did as he dropped her hand. As though she'd burned him. Or trapped him. "Are you okay?"

The tingling contorted into something dark and heavy. Full of rage and unpredictability. The trauma she'd suffered, the grief, the neglect, the outright hatred from her one surviving parent. The loss of her father and how she clung to those memories of their happy little family… Understanding struck. Her leveled reaction to getting pregnant, her asking him to be involved, her lack of any real relationships other than with her doctor friend and her boss. She'd…she'd played him from the beginning. His voice didn't sound like his own as he spoke and his heart rate catapulted into dangerous levels. "You got pregnant on purpose."

Chapter Twenty-Three

She'd expected this moment

She just hadn't expected it to hurt so much.

The nurse sat the ultrasound wand on the cart for cleaning and hit a couple buttons on the screen. Grabbing for a warm towel, she wiped it across Drennan's stomach to clean away the conductive jelly. "I'm going to print off a couple sonographs for you and give you two a few minutes of privacy."

Drennan couldn't feel her body apart from the cold sensation tightening the skin across her stomach. She registered the nurse leaving a strip of thin paper showing their baby on the counter and the door closing behind her, but nothing else would stay in focus. Her tongue felt too big for her mouth, a thousand different emotions clogging her throat. The first of which was a strong dose of disbelief. Followed closely by unfiltered anger.

Seconds passed in silence. Maybe a minute. She tried to breathe through the tears that came with extreme emotions but failed as she finally let herself look at him. Damn hormones.

"Tell me the truth." Muscle and tendon flexed in his forearms as he stared at her. That tightness traveled up the length of his arms and into his neck, hollowing his cheeks and the muscle ticking in his jaw. Harvey cut his gaze to the window—like he couldn't even bring himself to look at her—then back. "The night we slept together, you said you were on birth control. Were you lying?"

Her saliva felt more like a paste. "No."

It was all she could manage as her lungs threatened to burst. Those days leading up to their one night together had been a jumble of emotion and stress and adapting to this new life. She'd never meant for any of this. It'd just…happened, but she wouldn't apologize for it. She wouldn't apologize for the life growing inside of her. And she wouldn't regret it. Ever.

"So you admitting you've been waiting to get pregnant was just, what?" His gaze seemed to burn straight through her. Searching for a reason—any reason—to turn on her. "A colloquialism?"

Pain lanced through her chest. Not the kind anyone could see but just as damaging. The past three days played out in shards of memory—him bringing her back to his house to rest, making her food so she wouldn't pass out again, ensuring she made it home safely, staying the night in her bed. The words he'd said.

You're important to me.

I'm not going anywhere.

I'm not giving you up that easily.

Had it all been a lie? Why? Why go through that kind of effort if he'd been looking for a way out of their situation this entire time? She'd known his reasons for not wanting to be a father, but this wasn't past trauma talking. Accusing her of getting pregnant on purpose felt personal and cruel and…final. He didn't want her. He didn't want this baby, and he was ensuring he burned the bridge that'd been built over the past few days between them to ashes. Along with her heart. Drennan swallowed against the dryness in her throat, suddenly aware her lower half was still exposed by her lifted shirt and unbuttoned slacks. Where she could still feel the imprint of the backs of his knuckles when he'd helped her. She moved to fix her clothing and sat up on the exam table, the scream and crackle of hygienic paper beneath her too loud in her ears. Every sense she owned seemed to be on fire, too much. "Do you really think so little of me?"

"I think that maybe you aren't above using the same manipulation tactics that were used against you most of your life." He diverted his attention again, fueling that knot of uncertainty in her stomach. "Who better to wield them than a woman who has a literal encyclopedia of examples on her phone?"

She sucked in a sharp breath, the sting of which tore through the last few layers of her patience. And it was breaking her heart. She hadn't given a whole lot of thought to what a future between them might look like, but she'd wanted it. For them. For this baby. She'd wanted what she'd lost all those years ago. A family. Despite the red flags, his claims to not wanting to be a father, Harvey had shown her time and again that he cared. That there was something beneath the hard exterior that could make a different choice. And convinced her she was worth the effort. But she'd been wrong, and now she was pissed.

"Are you serious?" Drennan slid off the exam table. This was what he wanted. For her to get angry, to be the one to make the choice for him and give him a reason to leave, but she wouldn't do that. He had to be the one to say the words. No matter how much it might hurt hearing them, she'd let him. She'd let him walk away and never look back. Because anyone willing to throw her past in her face wasn't someone she wanted to be with. "After learning the reason why I don't tell people about what I've been through—that I'm afraid of people holding it over my head—you use it against me?"

He shifted his weight to ease the tension building with every word out of his mouth, but she wasn't the one who'd get hurt when it exploded. "You expect me to believe—"

Her laugh didn't sound remotely light or natural, and he had the audacity to flinch as though *she'd* struck *him*. But he'd started this. She would make damn sure he put the final nail in the coffin of their future together. That cold numbness she'd learned to don over the years descended. "Expect you to believe? I didn't have any expectations of you, Harvey. I have never asked anything of you. I didn't ask for you to drive me to the clinic after I passed out or for your offer to financially support this baby. I didn't ask you to come after me in those woods when I was abducted. You made your position about this baby clear, and I respected that. You made those choices. Not me. You. And I am grateful for them, really, I am, but not enough to let you treat me like this."

Harvey seemed to come back to himself right then. "Drennan, I—"

"No." She maneuvered around him, grabbing for her bag before heading for the door separating them from what was most likely an entire hall of eavesdropping nurses. "You more than anyone should know I could never manipulate another human being like I was manipulated, and the fact you're throwing that in my face only tells me one thing. You're a coward. You had the opportunity to move on from what's happened to you, but you're comfortable choosing a familiar misery. And I don't want any part of that near me or my child."

She grabbed for the door handle as the last dregs of anger drained out of sheer exhaustion. "I didn't get pregnant on purpose, Harvey, but there is not a single bone in my body that regrets this baby. I'm just sorry you do."

Wrenching the door open with a little more force than she expected, Drennan cringed against the solid wood colliding into the wall behind it. But she kept moving. Because if she stopped, she might never be able to put the distance between them she desperately needed right now. She didn't see the nurses who were most assuredly staring at her as she navigated down the corridor and through the lobby, and she didn't know where she was going as she hit the parking lot.

Damn it. Harvey had driven her to the clinic. Her car was... She didn't actually know. Back at her apartment? At the funeral home? She'd collected Ellender Garza's remains in the ME-sanctioned van before passing out in the park, so yes. She'd left her car in the funeral home parking lot. She could only imagine the amount of parking citations collecting under the windshield wipers after three days, but she'd have to worry about that later. Grabbing for her phone, Drennan headed south for two blocks. She wasn't going to wait in the clinic parking lot for Harvey to catch up to her. If she was being honest, she never wanted to see him again.

She didn't need his money. She didn't need his support or for him to have an interest in their baby's life. Not for birthdays or graduations or weddings. Not for weekend custody exchanges or family vacations. Her heart rate ticked up a notch. All she'd wanted was for him to choose *her*, but maybe her mother had been right. She wasn't worth the effort.

Wait. No. She knew better than to let that voice win.

What had Cassidy said? The bitch didn't get to live rent free in her head? Ugh. She was crying again. Swiping at her face, Drennan used her rideshare app to order a car to pick her up at the corner and climbed into the back seat when it arrived. No sign of Harvey, thankfully. "Metland Mortuary in Hurricane, please."

She didn't remember the drive. The chaos of thoughts— of what Harvey had accused her of, of her response, of the pain clawing deeper into her heart, the grief of a future she'd never have—it'd all blurred. Until she was climbing out of the car and heading for the front door of the funeral home. It was after hours. The director would be long gone by now, and Dr. Yarrow would've left around five. She'd lost track of the entire day between waking up to Harvey in her bed and the anticipation of seeing the baby on the ultrasound. Drennan pulled up short. "Oh, crap."

She'd left the sonogram photos at the clinic.

Well, they were gone now. Because she wasn't going back, and she wasn't going to ask Harvey if he'd picked them up. He'd most likely left them behind, and that just made her sad all over again. No. She wasn't going to think about that right now. Maybe when she got home and into a gallon-sized roll of egg-free cookie dough later. Then she'd let all this pressure out of her chest. Her key slid into the dead bolt and granted her access inside. The dim lighting overhead told her there wasn't anyone here tonight. While she probably should just collect the parking tickets, get in her car and go home, she couldn't ignore the need to check in on the Ellender Garza autopsy.

Dr. Yarrow would've finished the actual procedure within a few hours of starting, but there was a chance some of the toxicology results had come back. She just... she just needed to do something to help. Following the stairs down in the basement, she keyed in the six-digit number on the keypad securing the morgue before and after hours. There weren't too many times she'd had to use it, but Drennan had a feeling that wouldn't be the case for the next couple of weeks as the tension that'd crested back at the clinic refused to release. The green light lit up, and the thick steel doors unlocked.

She pushed through.

"Hello again, Dr. Hawes." Body heat pressed into her from behind. His mouth was beside her ear as he clamped a hand over her mouth. "I was hoping I would get to see you again."

Chapter Twenty-Four

He couldn't force himself to move.

Couldn't get a full breath.

The things he'd said to Drennan. The accusations he'd made...

Hell. Harvey closed his eyes mere seconds after she'd slammed the door into the wall. Shame unlike anything he'd experienced before burned beneath his skin. That familiar numbness had infiltrated his chest and refused to get out. It was a heavy feeling and he didn't have any desire to speak or move. All he wanted to do was close his eyes and sleep, because the process of breaking was exhausting. He'd tried to make the past few minutes justifiable, but no matter how hard he'd tried, he couldn't connect to that part of him he'd created to survive the worst.

Drennan had eviscerated it in a matter of days.

And that...scared the hell out of him.

The detachment wouldn't come as easily as it had in years past, and a sense of panic swirled up in its place. It was suffocating and dark and gut-clenching all at once. It closed in on him until he couldn't remember to breathe. Harvey fisted his hands at his sides, reaching for some tendril of control, but all he could think of was the utter devastation on her beautiful face.

Devastation he'd put there.

Because she was right. He was a coward.

He'd spent years not wanting a damn thing except to get through the day and the one after that, relying on his pain to drive his choices, counting on someone—anyone—to tell him what to do from one minute to the next. It was easier to live as a shell and isolate himself than to face the fact he might make a wrong choice. That he could put someone he cared about in danger just by being around him.

But Drennan had seen past that. She'd made him feel. She'd made him want. She was…everything. And he couldn't reach for that numbness because she'd made him feel everything for the first time in years. He couldn't go back. He felt her loss, an aching hollow sensation that threatened to bring him to his knees.

Then more.

The grief he hadn't let himself acknowledge when he got the news his mom had passed, a thing of its own that was heavy and full of rage. All the disappointment and heartache every time his father put his hands on him in anger, colder than he expected. The stab in his chest at the words he'd thrown in Drennan's face, burning and twisting.

He'd made this choice.

He'd made every choice that had brought him to this room, just as Drennan had said—not being able to distance himself, dreaming of a life that included her and the baby, hoping—and it was all going to destroy him from the inside out. She'd had every right to walk out on him, but Drennan would never hate him as much as he hated himself right then. But what was worse? The way he'd thrown her past in her face. Because she was right about that, too. She'd trusted him with one of her deepest fears, and he'd used it against her. He'd become his father in the worst way. Using someone's—a person he cared about—weakness against them to get what he wanted. To push Drennan away so thoroughly that there would be no going back, and it made him feel sick. No matter how many times he managed to apologize for that—if she let him get close enough to try—it would never be enough.

And he would have to live with that for the rest of his life.

He did this. He'd broken them and any kind of future he'd imagined between them, tried to break her. This caring, dedicated, strong woman who'd shown him the real meaning of healing. Harvey scrubbed his hands down his face. He needed to find her. Not for a second chance but to take back everything he'd said about her.

Because he knew she hadn't gotten pregnant on purpose. He knew she'd never use her experience with emotional abuse on anyone else for fear of them hurting themselves or others. And he knew he'd never deserved her. Never deserved a family of his own, to be happy. Hadn't his dad warned him a thousand times? That he was nothing and would always amount to nothing without his old man there to take care of their family.

Well, his dad had been right about that. At the first chance of making a different choice, Harvey had clung to that familiar misery because he could anticipate what happened next. He knew how his story would play out, but with Drennan? There had been too many variables and unknowns he couldn't see, even when he'd known it had to be better than his self-imposed suffering. Because she would've gladly been there.

If he'd just given her the chance.

But she didn't want him anywhere near her or their

baby, and he'd never hold that choice against her. He'd do what he could to support her from afar, whether she knew that support came from him or not. Send checks in the mail, drop off diapers and wipes and formula if she needed, ask his fellow rangers to help out so she could take a shower or a nap. Hell, he'd willingly learn how to knit or crochet a baby blanket if that was what she required.

Because Drennan deserved better. She deserved the world for how hard she'd fought to get the family she wanted.

Harvey peeled his eyes open, and the storm cycloning through him stilled. And took the air from his chest. The photos left on the counter pierced through the thick wall of shame and guilt crushing him in time to his racing pulse. He took one step closer, then another, his feet heavy as lead. Or maybe gravity had decided to kick his ass for what he'd done, too. He didn't care.

The gray and white patches on the dark background didn't mean a whole lot to him on the screen, but now, there were words on the photos marking exactly where the baby was growing. Their baby. Spindly limbs shot straight out from the middle of the gray-and-white outline, with another set coming out from the narrower end. Despite the mere eight weeks it'd been since that night in the bar, the baby's head had developed significantly, much larger than he'd expected. Echoes of that flutter—too fast and so loud—sounded in his head as he studied where he thought the heart might be.

It was a baby. His baby.

The rage he held on to for himself slowly lost its hold as he memorized the first photo. Harvey was careful as he peeled the line of photos off the cart. The paper was thinner than he expected—fragile—and he didn't want to do anything that might tear or damage it. Drennan would want them. Considering their conversation and the way he'd treated her, he imagined she'd left them behind by accident.

Logically, he'd known Drennan had been telling the truth about the pregnancy, but this... This made it real. He was going to be a father. His breath rushed out of him, eyes burning just for a second before he got himself under control. How the hell had he convinced himself he didn't want to be a part of this?

An ache set up in his shoulders. He wasn't sure how long he'd stood there or if the nurses in the corridor had called security to escort him out of the clinic. Hell, he wasn't even sure how long it'd been since Drennan had walked out, but he couldn't stay here. He'd driven Drennan to the clinic, and leaving her in the parking lot wasn't an option.

Folding the thin paper in thirds, each photo stacking on top of the other, he slipped the sonogram into his back pocket and headed for the cracked doorway. The nurses at the station outside the room eyed him with expressions of sadness and disbelief. All of which he'd earned. "Did you see where Dr. Hawes went?"

None of them answered, getting back to whatever clipboards and charts that needed to be filled out. Their collective anger pulsed against him, and he would take it. There was no doubt they'd heard every word—every accusation—he'd slung at Drennan, but he didn't have the energy to give it much thought. His father would've lashed out, embarrassed by the negative attention, but he was not his father.

A flood of something swept through him.

He was not his father.

Drennan had told him that, but he'd never really believed it. Until now. Every single decision he'd made to this point had been based on the opposite of what his dad would've done, but Harvey had never given himself that much credit. If his mother had dared to defend herself as Drennan had, his father would've ensured she wouldn't have been able to talk for a week. But he'd never let himself put his hands on the mother of his child. On anyone unless it was self-defense. And that… Recognizing that shed a weight from his shoulders he hadn't realized he'd been carrying for so long. Made him hope there was a chance to fix this. He wasn't his father. He never would be. Not with Drennan. Not with this baby.

"The woman who was in that room with me." Harvey clenched the edges of the upper level of the desk. He'd been an idiot to let her walk out of the exam room without him. She'd been abducted by an unknown suspect twenty-four hours ago. Hell, he'd given her his word he'd watch out for her, and only hours later, he'd broken that promise. "Do you know where she went?"

"She's not here." One of the nurses filed a folder in one of the cabinets. "She walked out the front doors after…" She cleared her throat. "I haven't seen her since."

"Where did she go?" Why did it suddenly feel like he couldn't take a full breath? "Which direction?"

Shaking her head, the nurse went back to her filing. "I'm sorry. I don't know."

Drennan was smart. She knew there was still a chance the man who'd abducted her wasn't finished with whatever plan he wanted to use her for. She'd go to someone she knew. Her doctor friend. What was her name? "Is Cassidy here? She's a doctor in the ER."

"Dr. Duffy?" Another nurse rounded into the station. "No. She's not on call today."

Hell. Then where would Drennan have gone? His skin prickled with unease. He'd driven her to the clinic. Without a ride, she would've requested a rideshare. But not home. Drennan was an expert in locking down her emotions and feelings to the point they might as well not exist. It was how she'd survived so many years under her mother's thumb, and as a former trauma physician, she would want to distract herself from sinking into that void. Which meant she'd most likely gone back to work. Alone.

Damn it. There was no guarantee she hadn't gone home to get as much distance from him as possible. He extracted his phone, scrolling through his received calls list as he headed for the front of the clinic. There was a chance he could catch up to her. That he could fix this. Harvey tapped Dr. Yarrow's information. It was after five. The medical examiner was most likely already home, but this couldn't wait. The line connected.

"Ranger Knight." Annoyance bled through the line. "I hope this is important."

Harvey didn't have time for small talk. "Have you heard from Drennan?"

Silence took a beat. "No. I assumed she was with you."

"She was." He shoved through the clinic's front doors and out into the parking lot. She wasn't here. "The autopsy for Ellender Garza. Have you issued your report?"

"I'm still waiting for the toxicology results." Dr. Yarrow didn't give him a chance to respond. "What is this about? Where is Drennan?"

Harvey scrubbed a hand down his face as failure ruptured from his insides. The same kind of failure he'd barely recovered from after hearing about his mother's death. He hadn't been able to protect her, but he couldn't fail Drennan. Or the baby. Desperation had him scanning the sidewalks and parked cars. Coming up empty. "I lost her."

Chapter Twenty-Five

Rough hands shoved her through the doors.

Drennan barely caught her balance as she was thrust into the exam room. Temperatures dropped on the other side of the doors, sinking through her slacks and T-shirt. All at once, she was aware of the presence at her back, the gun aimed at her head and the fact he'd blocked her from the only exit from the medical examiner's office. "You."

Her throat struggled with that single word.

"You're a hard one to pin down, Dr. Hawes." He moved into her line of vision, all too familiar and overbearing despite him being around the same height as Harvey. Except the man who'd knocked her unconscious and followed her into the backcountry had aged in a matter of days. The lines around his eyes and mouth had deepened, his cheekbones somehow more sunken. He'd shifted away from the doors, but there was no doubt he would catch her if she made a move he didn't want. "But I knew you wouldn't be able to stay away."

"What do you want?" Cold worked down into her lungs. While she'd become accustomed to working in the basement, this was different. Like a warning that forced tremors into her hands.

"I told you before." Only half of his mouth lifted into a

smile. "I need your help. Which one of these refrigerators is holding Ellender Garza?"

"I don't… I don't know." And she didn't. Dr. Yarrow had been the one to store her remains after the autopsy while she recovered from the abduction. Now that they had a positive ID for the victim, Dr. Yarrow would've ensured her family had been notified of her death. Once the autopsy was complete, they could take custody of the remains. She didn't even know if Ellender Garza was still here, but Drennan had a feeling his wanting to get to the body wasn't solely to say goodbye. "I would have to look at the paperwork, but why—"

"She has something I need." Her abductor collected a scalpel from a selection of tools laid out on one of the rolling carts Drennan spent her time as an assistant sterilizing and organizing for the ME. He seemed to study his reflection in the stainless steel.

Drennan's fingers ached for something—anything—she might be able to use as a weapon, but he'd positioned her between himself and Dr. Yarrow's desk. A stapler probably wouldn't come in handy right now. "We've done X-rays and collected her personal items. There isn't—"

Dread pooled at the base of her spine. There was something Ellender Garza's killer might want after her death, but the possibility was too much to consider.

His laugh punctured through the haze threatening to disconnect her from her body. He'd moved closer without her realizing, and Drennan took a step back. "You understand now, don't you?"

"The baby." Her mouth dried, and it took everything she had not to lift her hand to her own budding baby bump to assure her of the life she and Harvey had created. That nothing could hurt their baby. Giving away that kind of information—exposing her vulnerability—could put her more at risk than the scalpel in his hand. "You want her baby."

"Well, aren't you clever?" Pointing the scalpel in her direction, the killer took another step forward. "That baby is the last link between me and Ellender, and I will do whatever it takes to make sure it can't lead back to me."

"You're…" A monster. Emotion clogged her throat. It wasn't enough he'd taken Ellender Garza's life and the life of her child, he wanted to strip her of what could've been the victim's brightest hope. A wall of protectiveness slammed into place, drawing her shoulders back. He wasn't getting to that body or the baby Ellender had carried. She didn't know how she would stop him, but it felt important. Someone had to stand for the victim. Who better than someone who understood what it felt like not to have that support? Drennan's heart threatened to beat straight out of her chest as a single pained word escaped her control. "Why?"

He took another step, forcing Drennan back into the edge of Dr. Yarrow's desk. The overhead fluorescent lights glinted off something else on his hand, and her heart stopped beating for a breath. A wedding band. A full smile spread across his face. "Isn't it obvious? I love my wife."

Drennan clutched on to the edge of the desk with one hand, the other searching for something solid enough to protect herself with if necessary. She wanted to believe her abductor would let her go if she aided him in getting what he wanted, but that was a stupid, hopeful part of her that didn't match reality. She'd seen his face. Twice. And while neither the law enforcement rangers nor Springdale PD had been able to match his description to an identity over the past two days, that wasn't a loose end he could afford not to tie. "Your wife." Her chest tightened. "Ellender Garza wasn't your wife."

"No. She was not. She was a mistake, one my wife, the mayor, will never know about." He cocked his head to one side, seemingly trying to predict his prey's next move. Her being the prey. "So you can imagine how much I have at risk if that information got out, or if a federal database connects a murder victim back to me."

Drennan's hand connected with something heavy and smooth. The paperweight Dr. Yarrow's wife had gifted him on their anniversary this year holding a perfectly preserved black rose in the center. She covered it with her hand.

"Unfortunately, it's not as simple as losing my marriage." He maneuvered to her right, and she countered, losing the protection of the desk at her back. "My wife and I... It's been over for a long time. At least, on my end, but the National Park Service doesn't like to believe its rangers are capable of making base human choices like adultery. It's not good for public image. I'll lose my job, my connections and the very comfortable lifestyle I've built riding my wife's wealthy coattails, and you see, I just can't have that."

A shiver quaked down Drennan's spine. "You're a ranger?"

"No, Dr. Hawes. I'm *the* ranger, and I'm losing my patience, which is not great for you, as Ellender can attest." The superintendent. The man who ran the entirety of Zion National Park. Harvey's boss. "I recognized him, you know. That day in the backcountry. Ranger Knight lived up to his reputation. That is why I hired him after all, but his interest in you has interrupted my plans more than once, and well, I need this whole thing done with."

His tone sharpened. "Now show me where Ellender Garza is being stored."

Clutching the paperweight behind her back, she glanced at the wall of refrigerators. This was a small town. There weren't a whole lot of remains coming through that needed a medical examiner's review. "I don't know—"

He moved so fast, she barely had a chance to register it. The edge of steel pressed into the front of her throat as the wall at her back kept her from retreating. Her scream cut short as the killer clamped a hand over her mouth. "Then we're going to have to do this one by one, aren't we?"

Hot flares of fear and helplessness consumed her from the inside. Drennan squeezed her hand around the paperweight he had yet to notice as her survival instincts kicked in. She'd been in this position too many times to count. A victim, used, her well-being put at risk, and she hated it. She hated it with every fiber of her being as each cutting word from her mother's mouth or sent in a message dug deeper. Slicing her soul into even tinier pieces. And putting others first, making sure everyone else was taken care of in hope the smallest consideration was returned had only made it worse. Because here she was, once again putting herself between someone she believed needed to be protected and the threat. Ready to do what? Give up her life? Her baby's life?

No. Drennan wasn't okay with that.

She didn't want to teach her son or daughter that their needs should remain at the bottom of a priority list. She'd lived that life… It only ended in loneliness and resentment and rage that dictated every choice she'd ever made, and her baby deserved better. She deserved better.

Except once.

She'd made a choice of her own free will that night in

the bar. She'd chosen Harvey. For herself, to feel something other than all those crushing feelings of guilt from leaving her mother behind, grief from realizing she'd never have the relationship she'd always wanted with her last parent and fear from ending up alone.

And he'd been everything she'd needed that night.

Dominant but respectful, just enough to make her feel safe and taking the pressure off her of having to lead. Attentive and passionate, more so than any other boyfriend she'd been with. Understanding and committed, without any confusion about what they'd both sought that night. They hadn't spoken more than a handful of words in the hours they'd lost themselves to one another, but she'd never felt so connected to another person as she had him. She'd used him as thoroughly and completely as he'd used her, and for the first time since her entire world had been turned upside down, she'd felt...free.

Harvey had gifted her something no one else had. For just a night, she'd felt what it would be like to drop the responsibility she'd carried for everyone else's happiness but her own. Because adding hers to the mix had been too heavy and selfish. But he'd shown her how to put herself first, and she loved him for it.

Was *in* love with him for it.

Not just a culmination of one night or a baby, but because of all of it. The way he'd taken care of her after she'd passed out in the park, how he'd gone out of his way to ensure she ate and drank enough, urged her to get her rest. When he seemed more agitated with more distance between them and how he'd battled through his own demons to ensure her needs were met. But more, she loved the genuine care he put into making sure she and the baby were safe in the apartment…and from him. Abusers didn't do that. Neither did cowards.

Because, holy hell, she'd been wrong about him back in that office. Everything he'd done had been for her. At the risk of his job, his trauma and his future. Harvey cared about her, whether he realized it or not, and she'd let her own fears get in the way of seeing it. Until now.

"Move." Her abductor pressed the scalpel deeper, and a bead of blood slipped down her neck. "Toward the refrigerators."

The bite of pain dumped a dose of adrenaline into her blood, and Drennan had no choice but to do as she was ordered. For the sake of herself and the baby. "A lack of planning on your part does not constitute an emergency on mine."

His free hand bit into her arm as he jerked her to his side, pinning her hand with the paperweight against him as he maneuvered them to the other side of the exam room. Right before he shoved her ahead of him and into the wall of refrigerators. "Find her. Now."

Drennan seized the small bud of courage blooming in the center of her chest. Securing her hand around the paperweight, she gauged the distance between them. He could move fast. He'd already proven that, but he didn't know how far she would go for her child. "No."

She didn't give him a chance to recover, swinging the paperweight as hard as she could at his head.

The superintendent caught her wrist and squeezed the tendons there. Hard. The weight fell without her permission, shattering on the linoleum floor. "That was not a good choice, Dr. Hawes."

He lunged at her with the scalpel.

Chapter Twenty-Six

His fist nearly brought down the door.

"Drennan, it's me." Every cell in his body strained to pick up some kind of evidence that she'd come home after the doctor's office. Her car wasn't in the parking lot, and he'd already tested the doorknob and checked the windows to make sure they'd been locked. "Please. We need to talk."

She had every reason not to answer the door, but this wasn't about what'd happened between them. He just needed to know that she was safe. To settle the panic rolling through him in unending waves of acid and tightness.

Harvey knocked again. No answer. "I know you're upset, and you have every right to be. Just let me know you're okay."

But what if she wasn't? What if she couldn't come to the door because she'd passed out again or she was throwing up from the morning sickness? What if her abductor had intercepted her? Hell. She hadn't answered any of his calls or texts, and every second that passed without hearing from her was being etched into his palms by his fingernails. Dr. Yarrow hadn't seen or heard from her, and there was no way to tell if she'd gone back to the office, but the pathologist had hung up to reach out to the funeral director to check the security system.

"Damn it, Drennan. I'm sorry. For everything. For not supporting you when you told me you were pregnant and all that crap I said at the clinic. It wasn't true. I know that." His voice quaked as he recalled every vile accusation he'd used to put distance between them. He couldn't just stand here letting his head get the best of him. He had to get control of himself, keep himself level. For Drennan and the baby. Except that place of numbness he'd retreated to as threats arose over the years didn't exist anymore. "I just need you to open the door. Please."

Silence greeted him from the other side of the door.

"Screw this." Determination had him looking for a spare key she might've left in case she'd lost her keys or some other kind of emergency. He tossed her doormat and checked the fake plant up against the wall. He burned himself checking the top of the exterior light and got a splinter running his hand over the edge of her doorframe. No key. Frustration and pride battled to win his attention. He needed to get in. There was only one other option. In the name of concern. "I'm going to pay for this."

Harvey craned his head to one side and thrust his elbow through her front window. Glass sliced across the skin of his forearm and up his biceps, but he barely felt the pain as he reached through the pane for the lock on the window. It snapped to one side with his help, and he shoved the frame upward. In seconds, he'd gained access to the apartment. Which, he quickly realized, was in complete darkness. "Drennan?"

Could she be asleep? He doubted it considering the noise breaking the window had made. In fact, he wouldn't be surprised if one of her neighbors called the police. But he'd seen the exhaustion in her face and body language the past couple of days. The pregnancy was taking a toll on her, siphoning everything she had. He scanned the living room, everything exactly where he remembered, before heading into the bedroom.

Pushing the door open, Harvey went for the overhead light. He caught hints of her body wash, that light citrus scent that'd haunted him for weeks after she'd left his bed two months ago. She wasn't here, and a quick glance around told him she hadn't been for hours.

Tendrils of dread shot up his spine.

He'd started his search in the wrong location.

Backtracking through the apartment, he swept through the living room and went straight into the kitchen. His first instinct had been right. She'd most likely gone into work to lose herself in the case. What had she said? That she had to see this through. She had to finish the investigation into Ellender Garza's death. Hell. He'd wasted too much time coming here, but he'd needed to take the risk. He had no reason to believe she was in danger, just as when Dr. Yarrow had asked her to search for the victim's personal items at the scene, but that same sense of knowing—of urgency—took hold.

Harvey grabbed what he needed from beneath the kitchen sink and beelined for the window he'd broken. He wouldn't make it easier for anyone else to get to her. Duct taping the opening, he secured the broken window as best he could, a little concerned the police hadn't already rolled up in response to someone breaking in, but he'd worry about that later.

Walking out the front door, he gave her apartment one last glance. Praying with every nonreligious bone in his body that it wasn't the last time he saw it.

Tearing out of the parking lot, he navigated to the freeway and put the accelerator to the floor. The car accessory system lit up with an incoming call just as he hit the open road. Ranger Simpson. Harvey answered. "Yeah?"

"Wanted to let you know we got a hit on the gun you took off the kidnapper." The law enforcement ranger didn't wait for Harvey's response. "I've cross-checked the serial number with multiple federal databases and reached out to a friend in the Salt Lake Police Department, but nothing came back."

That didn't make sense. "You said you got a hit."

"I followed a gut instinct. The weapon you pulled off Drennan Hawes's kidnapper matches the make and model my law enforcement rangers are issued."

Every muscle down Harvey's back pulled tight. His fingers ached from the hold he had on the steering wheel. The oncoming headlights through the windshield filmed over with a red tint as anger overtook him. "You're telling me one of your rangers came after her?"

He filtered through the faces and names he'd collected over the years working side by side with the law enforcement division, but Harvey hadn't recognized Drennan's abductor when they'd come face-to-face.

"No. Every weapon I've issued to my rangers has been accounted for, but there is one that was issued outside of my division." Keyboard taps echoed through the line. "For the superintendent of the park."

"Pierce Shelton?" Confusion threatened to throw him into a spiral he might not ever come out of. "What the hell does a national park superintendent need with a federally-issued gun?"

"That's above my pay grade and long before I took over as head of this division." The key taps ended, and Simpson's voice lowered as though he needed to be careful of who overheard. "What I'm telling you is the serial number of the weapon you handed me matches the one issued to Superintendent Shelton."

Air escaped his chest. The red haze cleared—for now—but that part of him he'd always hated rushed to the surface, took control as a new outlet for all the hurt and pain and loss and isolation he'd suffered over the years was exposed. "Drennan was right, wasn't she? Ellender Garza wasn't married, but she'd gotten pregnant. By her killer. He killed her to cover it up."

Simpson shifted something around through the line. "But why go after Drennan? Does she know the victim or the superintendent? Did she see something she wasn't supposed to?"

The pieces were starting to fall into place, rocketing Harvey's desperation into dangerous levels. He couldn't push the SUV any faster without endangering his and other lives on the road, but his blood pulsed with need to get to her. Now. She was at the office. He had to believe that. Because if she wasn't—

"Because she's an assistant to the medical examiner. She has access to the remains." Harvey caught sight of the exit for Hurricane and took it as fast as he dared. "The Office of the Medical Examiner is a state agency with high-end security and data protection. The killer must need something from Ellender Garza's body. I'm guessing evidence that proves he's the father of the victim's baby. He had to have been waiting to see who would come back to the scene for evidence, and Drennan walked right into his ambush."

He'd come so damn close to losing her. Closer than he'd realized.

"You faced off with her abductor, took his weapon from him, and you didn't realize it was your boss who'd kidnapped her?" Simpson was moving now. Harvey wasn't sure why or where, but there was a chance he'd have the law enforcement division at his back. "Remind me not to look at your application to my division down the line."

Harvey slammed his palm against the steering wheel as he rolled through the empty freeway exit. "When was the last time you saw the superintendent in the park? And he wasn't the one who hired me. That was Risner—before he got fired for sexual harassment. Hell, I'd never met the man before."

But he would.

And it wouldn't end how he'd originally imagined meeting his boss.

Because there was no doubt in Harvey's mind the man who'd pointed a gun at him in the backcountry—who'd tied the mother of his child to a tree with intentions to hurt her—wouldn't walk away from this in one piece.

"What is your plan, here, Harvey?" The law enforcement ranger kept Harvey's head in the present. "If you go after the superintendent and we're wrong, you'll lose your job."

"We're not wrong." He didn't know how to explain his confidence, but the evidence was lining up. Whoever had taken Drennan had experience with wilderness survival and strategy, and the gun had been issued to the superintendent in the past. What were the chances a random abductor had gotten hold of it? Then again, what kind of criminal knowingly used a weapon that could be tied back to them? "I've got to go. I'm almost at the ME's office." The SUV's headlights coasted over the funeral home as he pulled into the parking lot. His nerves were tight. If he didn't get sights on Drennan in the next minute, he wasn't going to be able to breathe. "Drennan's not at home, and she's not answering her phone. I can't get ahold of her, and I'm worried something has happened."

"You're just telling me this now?" Simpson was breathing hard now as though he'd started sprinting. "I'll have Jordan take a run at the superintendent. See if she can track him down. I'm on my way."

The call ended before Harvey cut the engine. He wasn't law enforcement. He hadn't been issued an official weapon, but that didn't mean he was going in unarmed. Popping the glove compartment in the SUV, he extracted his personal weapon. Because there wasn't anything he wasn't willing to do to keep Drennan safe.

She was a healer, and Harvey was possibly the most broken person she'd ever met, but she'd somehow put him back together. Piece by piece, she'd helped him see the good he'd carried over the years instead of the bad. Good that had only come out for her, but it was there. He'd just had to look a little closer, to have a reason for it to come through. Drennan and the baby were that reason. She'd seen past the darkness he wielded as a shield. She lit him up, and he loved her for that. Wanted more of her in his life. Wanted to prove he wasn't his father, every day if she would just give him the chance. That he could be there for her, be there for the baby. He wanted to prove that he could make her happy if she forgave him. That he could love her the way she deserved.

Harvey checked the magazine in his weapon and slid it into the back of his waistband.

Ready to let go of the past. And claim his future.

Chapter Twenty-Seven

Pieces of Dr. Yarrow's shattered paperweight skidded across the floor as her abductor spun her around. Pain flared through her face as the superintendent who'd killed Ellender Garza pressed her into the wall of refrigerators from behind.

His body heated against hers, fitting them together in the worst way possible, and a surge of acid clogged her throat.

"I warned you what would happen if you didn't help me, Dr. Hawes." The scalpel he held nicked another patch of sensitive skin against her throat, and Drennan closed her eyes. She wouldn't cry. She wouldn't break. Not for him. "Open it."

She pressed her hands into the refrigerator door, bucking against him to add some semblance of distance between his front and her back. In vain. The killer only fought to hold her in place. "Get off me."

The words sounded strangled, even to her own ears. This wasn't how Harvey held her throughout the night. How his body heat had seeped into her muscles and soothed all the rough edges she'd picked up over the years. This was something dominating and manipulative and gut-nauseating. It felt as though thousands of spiders tiptoed across her skin, raising a rush of disgust.

The pressure at her back disappeared. Just for a moment. "Open it."

Drennan didn't have any other choice. She'd lost her only weapon. She didn't have the skills to fight back against a man almost double her size, and she wasn't about to risk the baby in an effort to escape. She was trapped. Her breath shuddered through her at the thought. Forcing her hands to peel away from the cold refrigerator door, she reached for the handle to her left. The door swung open, releasing a pillowy haze of mist. The morgue refrigerators leaned more toward freezers to slow decomposition of the remains they stored, and a chill tensed the muscles across her shoulders.

"It's empty. The next one." His command tightened around her rib cage. Sooner or later, they'd come across Ellender Garza. And then what? The scalpel was back at her throat, reminding her of how very little power she actually held in this room.

Drennan shifted over one row, grabbing for the refrigerator door. If she could get him close enough, there was a chance she could slam it in his face. Stun him long enough to make a run for the exit, but her abductor was being smart, keeping an arm's length between them. He'd see any move she made, and he'd punish her. He'd make it hurt.

She opened the next refrigerator, and the one after that.

Coming to the last in the row. She'd done what she could to stall, to think of a plan better than trying her luck at confronting the superintendent head-on, and now she was out of time. Her hands shook as she reached for the last door handle.

And swung it open.

A dark head of hair spread out across the sliding table stored inside the six-foot-deep refrigerator. The remains stored in the morgue no longer wore toe tags to identify them, but Drennan recognized the woman covered by a thin sheet inside.

"Pull her out." Her abductor moved in behind her. The scalpel sliced across her skin, and Drennan couldn't stop the gasp at the sting of pain.

She grabbed for her neck to gauge how deep he'd sliced, coming away with a slippery layer of blood. Nonlethal. He hadn't cut anything vital or she would've already been dead, but he'd gotten close. She was bleeding, and she'd continue to do so unless she added pressure.

"Now!" Pinching the back of her neck in one hand, he shoved her into the opening of the refrigerator.

Her entire body flinched from the violence in his voice. Stainless steel bit into her chest as she slapped her hands on the table to stop her momentum. The injury at her neck screamed as blood slipped beneath her blouse and across her collarbone. Drennan blinked against the sudden wave of dizziness. Whether it came from the drop in temperature, her pregnancy, the impact against the storage box or the laceration along the side of her neck, she didn't know. But she didn't have much time. "Okay." That single word sounded as though it'd come from a stranger. "Okay."

His body heat retreated for just a moment as he stepped out of her way.

Drennan tugged the tracked exam table toward her, her heart rate ticking too loud in her head. This...this wasn't how it was supposed to happen. It wasn't supposed to end like this. She was going to have a baby. She was going to be a mom with a family of her very own and turn everything she'd survived in her mother's house into something good.

She didn't want to die. Not before she had the chance to see her son or daughter grow up. To take their first breath and their first steps. She wanted the ridiculous kindergarten graduations and themed birthday parties and the constant "mamas" once her child learned how to talk. She wanted the scraped knees and the kisses that fixed them and the floods from the bathtub.

She could see it all. Right in front of her.

And Harvey... She could see him, too. Throwing his arms open for their toddler to run into at the end of a long workday, spinning around until they both got dizzy and sick. She saw him helping her with dinner and kissing the side of her neck where her abductor had sliced through the skin there. She could feel his hands on her hips and his calluses prickling goose bumps up her arms as if he was right here in the room with her.

It was so real...and so heartbreaking. Because Harvey couldn't love her until he learned how to accept and love himself, and she couldn't force him. She couldn't heal for him. But she could fight for them, for their family. However long it took, through whatever hardships that came. Whatever the risk or pain that most assuredly waited on the other side was worth it, wasn't it? He had to see that.

The exam table hit the end of the track, jarring the woman on the table. Drennan tried to back away. She'd given the killer what he wanted, led him straight to Ellender Garza. Her gaze flitted to the double steel doors. Could she make it before he lashed out?

The superintendent ripped back the sheet hiding the stitched Y-cut from both of the victim's shoulders, down over her sternum and into her belly. "Open her up."

Blood that hadn't seeped from her wound drained from her face. "What?"

"I told you what I came here for, Dr. Hawes." He extended the scalpel toward her, blade first. "And I'm not leaving without it. Open her up."

Her stomach pitched with a renewed flood of nausea. She shook her head. She'd cut into a thousand bodies over the course of her education and career, even as an assistant medical examiner, but she couldn't do this. "You can't be serious."

"What about me gives the impression that I'm joking?" He rounded the end of the cold exam table, closing the distance between them until she caught hints of his aftershave. Something gut-wrenching and cloying. "You're a doctor. You know what you're looking for. Get me my baby, and you walk away from this unscathed."

She tasted the lie as it seeped from his mouth. He'd let her see his face. There was no way in hell he'd let her leave this room alive. If she had to guess, he'd leave her body in one of the refrigerators to buy himself some time to escape. Drennan backed up another step. "Please. You don't have to do this. I can delete the DNA from the database. She can be buried or cremated. There are easier ways to get what you want. Don't make me do this."

His gaze narrowed on hers. "Now, why would a doctor beg me not…" Understanding smoothed the lines around his eyes, and his gaze dropped to her midsection. "Ah. So that's why Ranger Knight is so protective of you. You're carrying his baby. I had to wonder why a decorated soldier like that bothered to look twice at a boring as hell assistant ME in the middle of nowhere Utah."

The bite of pain that had nothing to do with the slice to her neck cut through her at his words. Boring. Unnecessary. Selfish. Disappointment. She'd heard the words a thousand times over, and they stung just as much coming from this complete stranger as they had from her mother.

Except Drennan had removed that particular tumor from her life. And she'd do it again. She'd do it as many times as it took. Because Harvey was right when he'd said she was strong. That she was important and that she deserved to be happy. And this son of a bitch was not making her very happy.

"I didn't say that." Drennan shifted her weight between her feet, ready to run as hard as her legs allowed. Would she make it far? Probably not. But she could go for one of the shards of paperweight on the floor.

A disjointed smile curled at one side of his mouth, as though he'd seen it on other people's faces and tried to replicate it himself in the mirror a thousand times, but it never made the full impact. Instead it curdled something in her stomach. "You didn't have to." He took another step, coming to her side of the table, no longer allowing anything to act as a barrier between them. "All right, Dr. Hawes. I'll make this easy for you."

Why did she have the impression he had no interest in making things easy for her? Her hands went clammy with him this close as every possibility played out in her mind.

Twisting the scalpel in one hand, he took that final step that put them toe to toe. "Either you get me what I want, or I take *your* baby."

Oxygen stalled in her chest. He wouldn't. Would he? Her chin wobbled as she forced herself to keep eye contact with the man threatening her child. Her future. No one would hurt this baby. She could do this. "I need a scalpel."

"Here." That smile was back, still a little off. "Take mine, but if you try to use it on me, I will do what I promised and leave you to bleed out on the floor."

Drennan took what he offered, the steel familiar and warm in her hand. "That's not going to work for me."

She struck, stabbing the blade of the scalpel into the soft tissue at the side of his neck, but adrenaline had thrown off her aim. She somehow managed to avoid hitting his carotid artery. The superintendent grabbed for his neck with one hand and backhanded her across the face with the other.

Drennan hit the line of refrigerators face-first. Lightning exploded behind her eyes just before she collapsed. She couldn't breathe, couldn't think.

"I warned you what would happen if you fought me, Dr. Hawes." Her clothing bunched around her neck as he fisted her collar and dragged her around the end of the exam table. He dropped her in front of another row of refrigerators, grabbing for the door. The table slid out next, and everything in her body went tight. No. No, no, no. He swayed above her, keeping pressure on his wound as he hauled her onto the exam table. "I always follow through on my promises."

Cold broke through the sweat along her spine. Drennan's sense of survival kicked in too late as he shoved the table back into the refrigerator. With her on it. She reached overhead for the door. Too late. "No!"

The lights cut out.

Chapter Twenty-Eight

Harvey kicked through the heavy double doors.

A mess of features contorted as Superintendent Pierce Shelton whipped his attention in Harvey's direction. He'd never met the man—hadn't seen anything more than his smiling photo in the monthly ranger newsletter—but every cell in Harvey's body told him this was the son of a bitch who'd attacked Drennan in the park. Who'd wanted to use her to get to the woman currently cut open on the table. Straightening, the superintendent seemed to gauge the distance between him and the door and conclude his chances weren't great. Now unmasked and exposed by the sharp fluorescent lighting overhead, Pierce Shelton's appearance exceeded his midlife age. More gray, more shadows to his face, more wear around his eyes. Not from exhaustion. *Desperation.* His hand shook as he pulled away from the victim on the table.

"Ranger Knight, what a pleasant surprise. I don't expect you're here for an update on the Ellender Garza case? Because I can confidently tell you the case is closed, and your services are no longer needed."

Harvey scanned the office, with its wall of freezers, Dr. Yarrow's desk shoved to one side, and the body Shelton stood over. Ice flooded his veins. *Drennan.* Where was Drennan? The rumble in his chest barely maintained a human effort as he took a step deeper into the morgue. "Where is she?"

A brittle smile spread across Shelton's face. "You'll have to be more specific."

"Drennan Hawes. The medical examiner you abducted." Her name grounded him in ways he'd never experienced before. No amount of meditation, centering or yoga had come close to the warmth her mere existence produced in his chest. Harvey took that next step.

"Doesn't ring a bell. Then again, I'm not familiar with the people in this office. I have rangers for that." Shelton shrugged, his mouth pinching with the effort. Every word out of this bastard's mouth wasted another precious second Drennan might not have. He was going to drag this out. Wanted Harvey to take whatever bait he spewed to buy himself time.

Which meant…

Harvey's gaze flickered to the rivulet of liquid spreading down the superintendent's uniform shirt. A metallic odor drove into Harvey's lungs. Blood. Shelton's? Or Drennan's? His knuckles screamed for relief as he fisted both hands. "Is that why you're bleeding all over the victim on the table? The woman you got pregnant then killed to cover the affair?"

There was a shift in the air between them. A different kind of unmasking. Charged with intention and an unleashed rawness. Shelton angled the scalpel in his hand down as he rounded the table. "Well, I guess there's no point in pretending any longer, is there? You know, I was hoping you were smart enough to walk away, but that's no longer an option. You'll just have to go in the freezer with her."

The freezer. Harvey's attention cut to the wall of horizontal freezers meant to preserve remains. Drennan… She was in there. She was dying. His lungs emptied of oxygen.

The distraction cost him.

Shelton charged, the lights glinting off the scalpel in one hand.

Harvey shot his fist straight into the superintendent's face. Pain ricocheted through the back of his hand and up his forearm, but he didn't stop. Couldn't stop. A groan bounced off the empty cream-colored walls as Shelton hit the linoleum. And still, Harvey didn't relent. One strike. Two. Three. Blood pumped a hard beat at the base of his throat. Hot and pounding. The scalpel was lost in the onslaught. The superintendent brought his forearms up to block the attack. A boot connected with Harvey's chest, and he lost the upper hand.

"And here I thought you had a future with NPS, Ranger Knight." Shelton shot to his feet. He swiped the blood dripping from his nose and mouth with the back of one hand. His left eye had started swelling under the spread of red inflammation, but the killer stood as though Harvey hadn't made a single dent. "Unfortunately, we're going to have to let you go."

Generations of rage and violence and lack of control flooded down Harvey's arms. *This.* This was what he'd tried to hide from Drennan. To protect her from. This was why he'd never wanted to be a father and had done so well in the military. In a matter of seconds, the fire he'd buried under years of denial and shame had been released in the face of losing the one person he'd never wanted to burn. It was like a physical presence embodied him—his father, his grandfather—as Harvey rocketed his fist toward Shelton's face. He would never allow this evil inside him to touch Drennan or their baby, but he'd let it out to save them. No matter the cost. He missed, swinging wide. He took another shot. Shelton ducked out of the way.

His third attempt landed home. His growl filled the morgue as the superintendent fell back into the medical examiner's desk. Office supplies and paperwork shot from the desk and over the floor.

He had to get to the freezer. Had to get Drennan out. Harvey lunged for the first hip-level door and nearly wrenched it off its hinges. Empty. He moved to the second. There weren't many options to choose from. Shelton would've had to have lifted her into the freezer with a seeping wound. One Drennan had most likely given him. "Hang on, baby. I'm coming. For both of you."

Again, empty.

"Where are you?" Cotton filled his head, undercut by a slow, steady pulse. As though he could hear her heartbeat through the metal, which wasn't possible, but every minute he wasted trying to take down Shelton slowed that pulse. She was running out of time.

Movement registered behind him.

Harvey lunged out of the way as the superintendent embedded the tip of a bone saw into the stainless steel freezer door. The bastard positioned himself between Harvey and the wall of freezers. Keeping him from Drennan. Shelton's shoulders rose and fell with exaggerated gasps, his blood pooling on the floor. "Did you really think it would be that easy, Knight? That you just get to live your happily-ever-after while I lose everything?"

That pulse in his head was getting slower. Softer. He was losing her. Her and the baby. Gauging the bladed teeth of the saw, Harvey closed the distance between them. Locking his hand around the superintendent's wrist, he vaulted Shelton's hand and the bone saw overhead and curled the blade back into the man's torso.

The saw cut straight through. Lodged in Superintendent Pierce Shelton's gut. One second. Two. That imaginary pulse had stopped. Harvey released his hold on the killer, and Shelton hit the floor. Alive. For now. Stepping over the bastard's prone body, he jerked the next freezer open. Then the fourth.

Air lodged in his throat as a head of beautiful hair escaped the confines of the freezer. He dragged the rolling table free and framed her too-cold face. Her eyes were closed, crystals clinging to her eyelashes as though her tears had frozen in place. Pressing his fingers to her throat, he almost collapsed in relief as her pulse kicked against his touch. Harvey pressed his forehead to hers. "I've got you, Drennan. I've always got you."

Chapter Twenty-Nine

His knuckles were already swelling.

Harvey shut down the pain in his hand as Dr. Cassidy Duffy took up position on one side of Drennan lying across the hospital bed. He hadn't known who else to call. Somehow it'd taken less than fifteen minutes for the doc to reach them in Hurricane, and he was never more grateful to see a physician than he was right then.

He'd almost been too late.

Harvey closed his eyes as he fisted the top blanket on Drennan's bed. The pressure had released some, but he could still see her, that lifeless thing he'd found in the freezer. Unmoving. Unresponsive. Drennan's skin had taken on a blue tint, her lips darker and her skin ice-cold. A section of her hair had broken straight off. He wasn't sure how long she'd been trapped, but the drop in temperature had obviously taken a toll. But she'd survived. He didn't know how. Anyone else would've given up, but she'd always been a fighter.

He locked down that sense of loss creeping into the edges of his mind as the pain in his knee flared to life. He'd pushed himself harder than he had in months, maybe years, these past couple of days, but he'd never regret a single moment. The monitor off to the side of her bed picked up every change in Drennan's heart rate. Strong and consistent compared to the first few minutes she'd been admitted to the clinic's emergency department. He soothed his thumb over the top of her foot, over and over until she'd realized where she'd been taken and that she was safe. Now she couldn't seem to detach herself, her foot following his retreat when he thought she might need space. Like she couldn't stand the thought of not touching him.

He felt the same, and he was prepared to stand by her all night if that was what she needed.

"Vitals are looking good. Your body temperature is almost back to normal." Dr. Duffy shone a penlight over Drennan's face, maneuvering it back and forth. "You'll live. Any pain?"

"Just on my neck." Drennan's voice sounded as though it'd been scraped over glass. A row of stitches lined a laceration along the side of her throat, black against her still too-pale skin. The son of a bitch who'd attacked her had taken a scalpel to her neck.

But she'd gotten him in the end. Well, her and the bone saw.

Superintendent Shelton had been aimlessly cutting into the dark-haired woman Harvey had pulled from the Emerald Pools when he'd arrived. Trying to take her baby, the only proof that'd he gotten Ellender Garza pregnant.

Both Ranger Simpson and Dr. Yarrow had chosen that exact moment to make their appearances and stop the superintendent from dying. The bastard was currently under arrest three cots down with a few new liters of blood and two law enforcement babysitters. Murder in the first degree and the attempted murder of a state official. As for Ellender Garza and her baby, Shelton had been cutting into her lower intestine rather than her uterus according to Dr. Yarrow. Police and law enforcement rangers had all the evidence they needed to connect the superintendent to Ellender Garza's death through DNA and motive.

Drennan's foot pressed into his hand, and Harvey snapped his gaze back to her. Intense green eyes locked on him as Dr. Duffy rolled back on her stool. He squeezed her foot, digging his thumb into the bottom to let her know he was still here. He wasn't going anywhere. She'd been through hell in more ways than one. Had to fight for her life alone against a man twice her size armed with a blade. She was lucky she hadn't sustained more serious injuries, and Harvey would thank a God he didn't believe in every day for that.

"I'm going to have her kept for observation overnight, and I want to get another ultrasound for the baby, considering the last twenty-four hours." Dr. Duffy turned her attention to him. "She needs rest and another round of fluids, but I think she'll be all right as long as she takes it easy. Can I assume you're staying with her?"

Harvey cleared his throat, not entirely sure if Drennan wanted him after their last conversation, but he nodded. "Yeah. I'm staying."

"Okay." The doctor shoved to stand. "I'll be back around to check on her in the morning."

"Thanks, Doc." He didn't just mean tonight. "For sticking with her all this time. Looking out for her."

A small smile transformed the overworked trauma physician as she patted Drennan's leg. "That's what friends are for. Call me if you need me."

Despite the chaos around the emergency room, silence pressed in on him as Drennan leveled that beautiful gaze on him. And, hell, he'd come so close to losing her. As much as he hated seeing her in this bed—again—he'd take this over never seeing her again. "You need water or something to eat? The cafeteria is just downstairs."

"No. Thank you." She clasped a hand on the stitches in her neck as she worked herself higher in the bed. "You don't have to stay. I'm sure there is literally anywhere else you want to be rather than here."

"I'm exactly where I want to be, Drennan." He moved to the head of the bed to help her with the pillow at her back. "And that's with you."

She didn't have an answer for that, but he could feel the hesitation to believe him in the silence that followed. She had no reason to believe him, and he didn't blame her. The things he'd said… "I lied to you."

"About wanting to stay?" Her eyebrows furrowed in the middle, right at the bridge of her nose, and it was so damn adorable the way she looked at him. Would their baby have the same look in a couple years? His chest tightened at the thought, but…he wanted to find out. "You can—"

"No. In the doctor's office. After your ultrasound." Harvey reached into his back pocket, pulling the roll of sonograms free. He smoothed the creases from all three pictures, trying to make up for the added damage they'd suffered during his fight with Superintendent Shelton. "I know you. I think you've let me see the real you more than you've ever let anyone before, and I took that trust and killed it."

She sucked in a sharp breath as she studied the sonograms in his hand, as though she didn't dare to move, wanting to see what he did next. Walking on eggshells. And, hell, he'd spent his entire life doing just that, and to see her have to react the same way… Harvey closed his eyes. He never wanted her to fear him.

"All those things I said about you getting pregnant on

purpose and using your mother's manipulation to get what you want, they were lies, Drennan." He handed her the sonogram images, a part of him hopeful there would be more that he could keep for himself, but for now, he had to let them go. "I don't believe for a second you would ever treat another human being the way you were treated since your dad died, and I'm sorry. You were right. I was being a coward. The way I acted? It was what my father used to do to my mother, and I never wanted to be that man. Ever."

She took the sonograms, running her fingers over the outline of their baby. "Then why did you say them?"

"Because I was scared." His pulse thudded hard in his throat. He grabbed for a corner of her pillow, strangling it beneath his hand as vulnerability stripped him bare. "I've spent a good part of my life detached and numb, but the second I set eyes on you in that bar, I knew you were going to mess up my life plan to die alone."

She looked at him then, and the entire world threatened to rip out from underneath his feet. She didn't look at him with anger or the same detachment he'd spoken of. He knew she was the kind of woman who could turn off her emotions and keep them off and that would be it. She'd already proven that by leaving her abuser behind and floundering for a new punching bag. Instead, Drennan looked at him with an openness he didn't deserve.

"Since meeting you, I've felt things I haven't in a long time. I've wanted things I've never wanted for myself before. A future. And seeing the baby on the ultrasound… I realized I was more broken than I wanted to admit, and just because you understood my pain doesn't mean my behavior was acceptable." His voice became gravelly as he tried to hold back. "But you saw all those pieces and somehow found a way to bring them back together. You didn't see the scars I've been using to keep people away. You just saw me. You made me feel seen, and for the first time in my life, I felt good enough for a brilliant, beautiful woman like you. Someone who I could spend the rest of my life with."

Tears glimmered in her eyes. Drennan swiped at her face. "Harvey—"

"I want you to keep messing up that life plan, Drennan." Harvey slid his free hand across her middle, right where their baby was growing. "You and this baby. I love you. I'm ridiculously in love with you. Please forgive me. Please give me another chance to prove I can be there for you." He cleared his throat. "That I can be a good father."

That brilliant smile that'd always made his heart stop flashed wide. Drennan slid her hand over his, over her nonexistent baby bump. "Does that mean you're going to be there for all my future ob-gyn appointments?"

"Every appointment. Every time you have to throw up. Late-night grocery store runs for food cravings. Massaging your feet when they get swollen and sore." Harvey leaned down, his mouth hovering over hers. "Babyproofing the entire house. Lamaze classes. Learning about breastfeeding. I want to be there for the birthday parties and the Christmases and Thanksgivings. I want the graduations and weddings and proms. I want it all."

Her breath shuddered through her, and the monitor tracking her heart rate ticked higher. Drennan dropped her gaze to his mouth and back, and a searing heat lightninged through him. "And if I wanted you to be more than a supportive father?"

Hell. This woman was going to break him in an all new way, and Harvey had the sense he'd enjoy every second of it. "More?"

"More." She nodded, her bottom lip brushing against his. "Because I'm in love with you, too. I think I fell in love with you the night we met. But I've spent my whole life dreaming of family that loves me, Harvey, and I'm not willing to settle for scraps anymore. Can you give me that?"

"For the rest of my life." Nothing could've stopped him from kissing her then. Harvey crushed his mouth to hers, careful of her injuries and the fact she'd been through so much in the past few days. Her mouth parted at his insistence, and he drank her in. "I told you before, Dr. Hawes. You're mine. Forever."

She smiled against his mouth, slipping an arm around his neck to pull him onto the bed with her. "Forever, Ranger Knight."

* * * * *

Get up to 4 Free Books!

We'll send you 2 free books from each series you try PLUS a free Mystery Gift.

FREE Value Over **$25**

Both the **Harlequin Intrigue®** and **Harlequin® Romantic Suspense** series feature compelling novels filled with heart-racing action-packed romance that will keep you on the edge of your seat.

YES! Please send me 2 FREE novels from the Harlequin Intrigue or Harlequin Romantic Suspense series and my FREE gift (gift is worth about $10 retail). After receiving them, if I don't wish to receive any more books, I can return the shipping statement marked "cancel." If I don't cancel, I will receive 6 brand-new Harlequin Intrigue Larger-Print books every month and be billed just $7.19 each in the U.S. or $7.99 each in Canada, or 4 brand-new Harlequin Romantic Suspense books every month and be billed just $6.39 each in the U.S. or $7.19 each in Canada, a savings of 20% off the cover price. It's quite a bargain! Shipping and handling is just 50¢ per book in the U.S. and $1.25 per book in Canada.* I understand that accepting the 2 free books and gift places me under no obligation to buy anything. I can always return a shipment and cancel at any time by calling the number below. The free books and gift are mine to keep no matter what I decide.

Choose one:
- ☐ **Harlequin Intrigue Larger-Print** (199/399 BPA G36Y)
- ☐ **Harlequin Romantic Suspense** (240/340 BPA G36Y)
- ☐ **Or Try Both!** (199/399 & 240/340 BPA G36Z)

Name (please print)

Address   Apt. #

City   State/Province   Zip/Postal Code

Email: Please check this box ☐ if you would like to receive newsletters and promotional emails from Harlequin Enterprises ULC and its affiliates. You can unsubscribe anytime.

Mail to the **Harlequin Reader Service:**
IN U.S.A.: P.O. Box 1341, Buffalo, NY 14240-8531
IN CANADA: P.O. Box 603, Fort Erie, Ontario L2A 5X3

Want to explore our other series or interested in ebooks? Visit www.ReaderService.com or call 1-800-873-8635.